D0363813

WANTED:
ROYAL WIFE
AND MOTHER

WANTED:
ROYAL WIFE
AND MOTHER

BY

MARION LENNOX

MILLS & BOON®

Pure reading pleasure™

First published in Great Britain 2008
Large Print edition 2008
Harlequin Mills & Boon Limited,
Eton House, 18-24 Paradise Road,
Richmond, Surrey TW9 1SR·

ISBN: 978 0 263 20102 4

Set in Times Roman 16½ on 18¼ pt.
16-1208-54808

Printed and bound in Great Britain
by CPI Antony Rowe, Chippenham, Wiltshire

With love and grateful thanks to the Maytoners.
True friends are gold. Or should that be opals?

CHAPTER ONE

IT WAS the end of a long day in the goldfields, and Kelly had personally found almost a teaspoon of gold. The slivers of precious metal were now dispersed into scores of glass vials, to be taken home as keepsakes of a journey back in time.

Her tourists were happy. She should be, too.

But she was wet. She was dressed in period costume and raincoats hadn't been invented in the eighteen-fifties. As the day had grown colder Kelly had directed her tour groups down the mines, but she'd been wet before she'd gone down and the cold had stayed with her. Now she emerged from underground, desperate to head to her little cottage on the hill, strip off her dungarees and leather boots and sink into a hot bath.

She might be a historian on what was the re-creation of a piece of the Australian goldfields but, when it came to the offer of a hot bath, Kelly was a thoroughly modern girl.

The park horses—a working team that tugged a coach round the diggings during the day—lumbered up the track towards the stables and she stood well back. Horses... Once she'd loved them, but even now, after all this time, she hated to go near them. She waited.

Once the horses passed she expected her way home to be clear, but there were always one or two tourists lagging behind, as eager to stay as she was eager to leave. She had to manoeuvre her way past a last couple. A man and a child. They seemed to have been waiting for the horses to pass so they could speak to her.

Who were they? She hadn't seen them on the tour and she'd surely have noticed. The guy was strikingly good-looking: tall, tanned, jet-black hair—aristocratic? It was an odd description, she thought, but it seemed strangely appropriate. He was lean and strongly boned. Almost...what was the word... aquiline?

The little boy—the man's son?—was similarly striking, with olive skin, glossy black curls and huge brown eyes. He looked about five years old, and the sight of him made Kelly's gut clench as it had clenched countless times over the past five years.

How many five-year-old boys were there in the world?

Could she ever move on?

Could this be her?

Rafael stared across the track at the slip of a girl waiting for the horses to pass. Princess Kellyn Marie de Boutaine of Alp de Ciel? The thought was laughable.

She was wet, bedraggled and smeared with mud. She was dressed like an eighteen-fifties gold-miner, only most eighteen-fifties gold-miners didn't have chestnut curls escaping from under their felt brimmed hats.

He'd read the report. This had to be her.

But this was harder than he'd thought.

Back home it had seemed relatively straightforward. He'd been appalled when he'd received the investigative report. Like the rest of the population of Alp de Ciel, he'd thought this woman was a…well, no fit mother for a prince. He'd thought she'd left of her own free will, as unwilling to commit to her new baby as her royal husband had been.

But what the report had told him…

He cast a glance down at the child at his side. If the report was true… If she'd been forced away…

He had to step forward. If he did only this one thing as Prince Regent, it had to be the righting of this huge injustice.

Mathieu was gripping his hand with a ferocity that betrayed his tension. They'd come all this way. The child couldn't be messed around.

The woman—Kellyn?—was about to leave. The park was about to close.

This had to be done now.

The horses were gone and yet they were still here. Man and child. Watching her.

'Can I help you?' Kelly managed, forcing forward her stock standard I'll-make-you-enjoy-your-experience-here-or-bust smile that most of the staff here practised eternally. 'Is there anything you need to know before we lock up for the night? I'm sorry, but we are closing.'

The rest of the group were moving away, making their way towards the exit. Pete, the elderly security guard, was leaning on the gates, waiting to close.

'I can give you a booklet with pictures of the

diggings if you like,' she offered. She smiled down at the child, trying really hard not to think how like…how like…

No. That was the way of madness.

'I see you came late,' she said as the child didn't answer. 'If you like, we can stamp your tickets so you can come back tomorrow. It's not much extra.'

'I'd like to come back tomorrow,' the child said gravely, with the hint of a French accent in his voice. 'Can we, Uncle Rafael?'

'I'm not sure,' his uncle replied. 'I'm not actually sure this is who we're looking for. The guy on the gate…he said you were Kellyn Marie Fender.'

Her world stilled. There was something about this pair… There was something about the way this man was watching her…

'Y…yes,' she managed.

'Then we need to talk,' he said urgently and Kelly cast a frantic glance at Pete. She was suddenly terrified.

'I'm sorry,' she managed. 'The park's closing. Can you come back tomorrow?'

'This is a private matter.'

'What's a private matter?'

'Mathieu is a private matter,' he said softly, and

he smiled ruefully down at the little boy by his side. 'Mathieu, this is the lady we've come to meet. I believe this lady is your mother.'

The world stopped. Just like that.

Death was the cessation of the heart beating and that was what it felt like. Nothing moved. Nothing, nothing, nothing.

She gazed at the man for a long moment, as if she were unable to break her gaze—as if she were unable to kick-start her heart. She felt frozen.

There'd been noises before—the cheerful clamour of tourists heading home. Now there was nothing. Her ears weren't hearing.

She put a hand out, fighting for balance in a world that had suddenly jerked at a crazy angle. She might fall. She had to get her heart to work if she wasn't to fall. She had to breathe.

The man's hands came out and caught her under the elbows, supporting her, holding her firm, forcing her to stay upright.

'Kellyn?'

She fought to get her next breath.

Another. Another.

Finally she found the strength to stand without support. She tugged away a little and he released her, watching her calmly as she took a couple of dazed steps back.

They were both watching her, man and boy. Both with that same calm, unjudging patience.

Could she see…could she see?

Maybe she could.

'Mathieu,' she breathed, and the child looked a question at the man and nodded gravely.

'*Oui.*'

'*Parlez-vous Anglais?*' she asked for want of anything more sensible to ask, for she'd already had a demonstration that he did, and both man and boy nodded.

'*Oui,*' the little boy said again. He reclaimed his uncle's hand and held tight. 'My Aunt Laura says it's very important to know *Anglais.*'

'Mathieu,' she breathed again, and her knees started to buckle again. But this time she was more in control. She let them give, squatting so she was on the child's level. '*Tu est Mathieu. Mon…mon Mathieu.*'

The little boy hesitated. He looked again at his uncle. Rafael nodded—gravely, definite—and the little boy looked again at Kelly.

He kept on looking. He was taking in every inch of her. He put a hand out to touch her dungarees, as if checking that they were real. He looked again at her face and his small chin wobbled.

'I don't know,' he whispered.

'You do know,' Rafael said gently. 'We've explained it to you.'

'But she doesn't look…'

Kelly had forgotten to breathe. It seemed the child was as terrified as she was. And as unbelieving. He blinked a couple of times and a tear rolled down his cheek, unchecked.

She had an urgent need to wipe it away. To touch him.

She mustn't. She mustn't even breathe. She had to wait.

And finally he came to a decision. He gulped a couple of times and gripped his uncle's hand as if it were a lifeline. But the look he gave her… There was desperate hope as well as terror.

'Uncle Rafael says you are my mama,' the child whispered.

And that was the end of her self-control. She, who'd sworn five years ago that she was done crying, that she'd never cry again, felt tears slip helplessly down her cheeks. She couldn't stop them—she had no idea how to even try. She couldn't think what to do, what to say. She simply squatted before her son and let the tears slip down her cheeks.

'Oi! Kelly.' It was Pete on the gate, concerned at her body language, concerned to get these stragglers out of the park. 'It's five past five,' he yelled.

Rafael glanced down at Kelly, who was past speaking, and then called to Pete, 'We're not tourists. We're friends of Kellyn's.'

'Kelly?' Pete called, doubtful, and Kelly somehow stopped gazing at Mathieu, gulped a couple of times and found the strength to answer.

'Lock up, Pete,' she called unsteadily. 'I'll let them out through the cottage.'

'You sure?' Pete sounded worried. The head of security was a burly sixty-year-old who lived and breathed this park. He also treated the park employees as family. Any minute now he'd demand to see Rafael's credentials and give Kelly a lecture on admitting strange men into her home.

'It's okay,' Kelly called, straightening and forcing her voice to sound a lot more sure than she felt. 'I know…I know these people.' Her voice fell away to a whisper. 'I know this child.'

The park—a restoration and re-enactment of life on the goldfields in the eighteen-fifties—

had mine-shafts, camps, shops, hotels and also tiny homes. As much as possible it was a viable, self-supporting community and the homes were lived in.

Kelly's cottage was halfway up the hill. There were ten of these cottages in the park, and Kelly felt herself lucky to have one. It might not have mod cons but it had everything she needed and she could stay steeped in history and hardly ever step out into the real world.

Which was the way she liked it. She didn't think much of the outside world. Once, a lifetime ago, she'd ventured a long way out and been so badly hurt she might never venture out again.

Now she stepped through the front door of her cottage feeling as if her world were tipping. The warmth of her wood-stove reached out to greet her, and it was all she could do not to turn round and slam the door behind her before these strangers followed her in.

For the more she thought about it, the more she thought this must be some cruel joke. Fate would never do this to her. Life had robbed her of Mathieu. To hand him back… It was an unbelievable dream that must have no foundation in reality.

But here they were, following close on her

heels, allowing her no time to slam the door before they entered.

The child's gaze was everywhere, his eyes enormous, clearly astonished that behind the façade of an ancient weatherboard hut was a snug little home. There was no requirement by the park administration that the interiors were kept authentic but Kelly loved her ancient wood-stove, her battered pine table, the set of kangaroo-backed chairs with bright cushions tied to each and the overstuffed settee stretched out beside the fire.

She had soup on the stove—leek and potato— and the smell after a cold and bleak day was a welcome all by itself.

Now they were inside, she didn't know where to start. The man—Rafael—was watching her. She watched the child. Mathieu watched everything.

'Is this where you live?' the little boy asked at last. He was backing away from eye contact with her now. The mother-child thing…neither of them knew where to start.

'Yes.' She couldn't get enough of him. She didn't believe—yet—but she wanted to, oh, she wanted to, and for this tiny sliver of time she thought what if…what if?

'Do you have a real stove?'

'This is a real stove. Do you want to see the fire inside?'

'Yes, please.'

She flicked open the fire door. He stared at the pile of glowing cinders and frowned.

'Can you cook on this?'

'You can see the pot of soup.' She lifted a log from the hearth and put it in. 'My fire made my soup. It's been simmering all day. Every now and then I've had to pop home to put another log on.'

'But you must have a stove with knobs. Like we have in the palace kitchens.'

The palace kitchens. Alp de Ciel. Maybe... maybe...

'I do have an electric stove,' she said cautiously, feeling as if she were buying time. She opened a cupboard and tugged out a little electric appliance—two hotplates complete with knobs. 'In summer when it's really hot I cook with this.'

'But in winter you cook with fire.'

'Yes.'

'It's very interesting,' Mathieu said, while Rafael still watched and said nothing. His gaze disconcerted her. She wanted to focus exclusively on Mathieu but Rafael had unnerved her.

'Does it cook cakes?' Mathieu asked.

'There's a cake in the pantry,' she said. She'd been miserable last night and had baked, just for the comfort of it. There'd been a staff meeting planned for this morning and she'd intended to take it along, but then one of the guides had called in sick and she'd had to take his place. So the cake was intact.

She produced it now while the child watched with wide-eyed solemnity and the man kept watching her.

'It's chocolate,' Mathieu breathed.

'Chocolate's my favourite,' Kelly admitted.

'Uncle Rafael says you're my mother,' Mathieu said, still not looking at her but eyeing the cake as if it might give a clue to the veracity of his uncle's statement.

'So he does.'

'I don't really understand,' Mathieu complained. 'I thought my mother would wear a pretty dress.'

It was too much. Kelly stared at the child and she thought she was crazy, this was crazy, there was no way this was real.

I thought my mother would wear a pretty dress.

This little one had a vision of his mother. As she'd had a vision of her child.

'I feel like crying,' she said to the room in general, thinking maybe that saying it might ward it off. But shock itself was stopping her from weeping. Every nerve in her body was focused exclusively on this little boy.

'I don't understand either,' she said at last as both males looked apprehensive. They were also looking a little confused. No, she wasn't wearing a dress. She was wearing dungarees and a flannel shirt and leather boots. She was caked in mud. She was no one's idea of a mother.

She hadn't been a mother for five years.

'You know Mathieu's father is dead?' Rafael said gently, and her eyes jerked up to his.

'Kass is dead?' She stared wildly at him and then looked down at the little boy again. 'Your papa?'

'Papa died in a car crash,' Mathieu said in a matter-of-fact voice.

'Matty, I'm so sorry.'

Matty. The name Mathieu had been chosen by his father. It had seemed far too formal for such a scrap of a baby. Matty was what she'd called him for those few short weeks…

'Aunt Laura calls me Matty,' he said, sounding pleased. 'Aunt Laura says the nurses told her my mama called me Matty.'

'But…' Her head was threatening to explode. She sank on to a chair because her legs wouldn't hold her up any more. 'But…'

'Matty, why don't you do the honours with the cake?' Rafael suggested. With a sideways glance at Kelly—who was far too winded to think about answering—he opened the cutlery drawer, found a knife blunt enough for a child to handle, found three plates and set them on the side bench. 'Three equal pieces, Matty,' he said. 'You cut and we'll choose. As wide as your middle finger is long.'

Matty looked pleased. He crossed to the bench and held up his middle finger, carefully assessing. Clearly cake-cutting would take a while.

Rafael pulled out a chair and sat on the opposite side of the table to Kelly. He reached over, took her hands in his and held them. He had big hands. Callused. Work worn. They completely enclosed hers. Two strong, warm hands, where hers were freezing. She must be freezing, she thought. She couldn't stop shivering.

She'd had the flu. She wasn't over it yet. Maybe that was why she was shivering.

'I should have phoned,' he said ruefully. 'This has been too much of a shock. But I was sure you'd have heard, and I didn't understand why you didn't contact us.'

'It's me who doesn't understand,' she whispered.

'You don't read the newspapers?'

'I…not lately. I've been unwell. This place has been hopelessly understaffed. What have I missed?'

'Alp de Ciel is only a small country but the death of its sovereign made worldwide news. Even right down here in Australia.'

'When?' What had happened to her voice? It was coming out as a squeak. She tried to pull her hands away but failed. She couldn't stop this stupid shivering.

He was still holding her. Maybe he thought she needed this contact. But he was a de Boutaine. Part of her life that had been blocked out for ever.

Matty was a de Boutaine. Matty was in her kitchen cutting cake.

'I've had flu,' she whispered, trying to make sense of it. 'Real flu, where you don't come out from under your pillow for weeks. The whole park staff's been decimated. For the last couple of months, if we haven't been sick we've been run off our feet covering for those who are.'

'Which is why you're trudging round in the mud,' he said softly. 'My informants say you're a research historian here.'

His informants. That sounded like Kass. 'What I do is none of your business,' she snapped.

'The woman who is responsible for Mathieu is very much my business.'

She stared at him. Staring seemed all she was capable of. There was nothing else to do that she could think of.

'Who…who are you?' she whispered.

'Kass was my cousin.'

She moistened her lips. 'I don't think…I never met…'

'Kass and I didn't get on,' he said, with a sideways warning glance at Matty. There were things that obviously couldn't be said in Matty's presence. But Matty was doing his measuring and cutting with the focus of a neurosurgeon. These cake slices would be exactly equal if it took him half an hour to get it right.

'My father was the old prince's younger brother,' Rafael said. 'Papa married an American girl—my mother, Laura—and we lived in the dower house at the castle. My father died when I was a teenager, but my mother still lives at the castle. She and my father were very happy and she never wants to leave, but I left when I was nineteen. For the last fifteen years I've spent my life in New York. Until Kass died. Then I was called on. To my horror, I've discovered I'm Prince Regent.'

'Prince Regent.'

'It seems I'm the ruling Prince Regent of Alp de Ciel until Matty reaches twenty-five,' he said ruefully. 'Unless I knock it back. Which I don't intend to.'

So the Prince Regent of Alp de Ciel was sitting at her kitchen table. Unbelievable. She didn't believe it. She was fighting a mad desire to laugh.

How close to hysterics was she?

'So you're Prince Regent of Ciel.'

'Yes.'

'And you've come to Australia…why?'

'Because Matty needs his mother.'

That was enough to take her breath away all over again.

'Kass decreed he didn't need his mother five years ago,' she whispered. She shot Matty a quick glance to make sure he wasn't a figment of imagination. She'd been delirious for twenty-four hours with influenza. She was still as weak as a kitten. This was surely an extension of her illness.

But no. Matty was here. He was evening up his slices, taking a surreptitious nibble of an equalizing sliver.

'My cousin,' Rafael was saying, softly so the words were for her alone, 'had the morals of a sewer rat. I heard what he did to you. You were a kid; he married you and then you were in no man's land. Mother of a future Crown Prince. Only of course you'd signed your rights away. As a commoner marrying into royalty, you had to sign an agreement saying if the marriage ever broke down full custody of any children would stay with the Crown. So when you had an affair…'

'I had no affair,' she said, dragging desperately on to truth as a lifeline.

'It seems now that you didn't,' Rafael said grimly. 'It was the only thing that made it palatable to the world. That there were men who claimed to be your lovers. That you were proven to be immoral. Everyone knew Kass never had any intention of being faithful to a wife—he only married you to make his father furious. But…'

'I don't want to talk about this.'

'No, but you must.' His hands were still

holding hers. She stared down at the link. It seemed wrong but it was such an effort to pull away. Did she have the strength?

Yes. This man was a de Boutaine. She had no choice. She tugged and he released her.

'The story as I knew it,' he said softly, 'is that Kass married a commoner who was little better than he was. Together you had a child, but the only time you came to the castle was in the last stages of your pregnancy. By the time you had the child, the word was out. Your behaviour was said to be such that the marriage could never work. Kass's public portrayal of your character was so appalling he even insisted on DNA testing to prove Mathieu was his son. Then, once Mathieu was proven to be his, he sent you out of the country. He cancelled your visa and he didn't allow you back. The terms of the marriage contract left you no room to fight, though the people of Alp de Ciel always assumed you were well looked after in a monetary sense. You disappeared into obscurity—not even the women's magazines managed to trace you. You weren't a renowned beauty looking for publicity. You weren't flying to your lawyers to demand more money. You simply disappeared.'

'And Matty?' she whispered. For five years… every minute of every day he'd stayed in her heart. What had been happening to him?

But Rafael was smiling. Matty had the three slices even now, but there'd been a few crumbs scattered in the process. He was carefully collecting them, neatening the plates before he presented his offering to the adults.

'Matty's been luckier than he might have been,' Rafael told her. 'Kass couldn't be bothered with him and abandoned him to the nursery. My mother had been in the US with me for the few weeks while you were at the castle—she knew nothing about you, and as far as she was concerned the reports about you were true—but when she returned there was a new baby. He had no mother and a father who didn't care. My mother loves him to bits. Every summer when Kass closed the palace and disappeared to the gambling dens in Monaco or the South of France, she brought him to New York to stay with me. Kass didn't care.' He smiled. 'My mother cares, though. Which is where I come into the picture.'

There were too many people. There was too much information. 'My head hurts,' she managed.

'I imagine it must,' he said and smiled again, a gentle smile of sympathy that, had she not been too winded to think past Matty, might have given her pause. It was some smile.

'My mother took Kass's word for what sort of woman you were,' he said. 'We knew Kass had married to disoblige his father and that he'd married a…well, that he'd married someone really unsuitable seemed entirely probable. When Kass told the world how appalling you were he was believed—simply because to marry someone appalling was what he'd declared he'd do. You disappeared. The lie remained. Then, when Kass died, his secretary finally told me what really happened.

'Crater…'

'You remember Crater?'

'Yes.' All too well. An elderly palace official—the Secretary of State—with an armful of official documents, clearly spelling out her future. He'd sounded sympathetic but implacable. Telling her she had no rights to her son. Showing her the wording of the documents she'd signed in a romantic haze, never believing there could be any cause to act on. Telling her she had no recourse but to leave.

'He's felt appalling for five years,' Rafael told her. 'He said that six years ago Kass left the castle, furious with his father, and met you working on site on an archaeological dig. He said you were pretty and shy and Kass almost literally swept you off your feet. He could be the most charming man alive, my cousin Kass. Anyway, as far as Kass was concerned you fitted the bill. You were a nobody. You had no family. He married you out of hand, settled you in France and made you pregnant. Only then, of course, his father died. Kass was stuck with a wife he didn't need or want. So he simply paid his henchmen to dig up dirt on you—make it up, it now seems. Crater had doubts—he was the only one who'd met you before you were married when Kass had called on him to draw up the marriage documents—but there was little he could do. The prenuptial contracts were watertight and you were gone before he could investigate further.'

'Yes…' She remembered it every minute of her life. A paid nanny holding the baby—her baby. Matty had been four weeks old. Kass, implacable, scornful, moving on.

'I'm cancelling your visa this minute, you

stupid cow. You won't be permitted to stay. Stop snivelling. You'll get an allowance. You're set up for life, so move on.'

She'd been so alone. There had been a castle full of paid servants but there had been no one to help her. She remembered Crater—a silver-haired, elderly man who'd been gentle enough with her—but he hadn't helped her, and no one else had as much as smiled at her.

She had to go, so leave she had. And that had been that. She'd gone back to France for a while, hoping against hope there'd be a loophole that would allow her access to her little son. She'd talked to lawyers. She'd pleaded with lawyers, so many lawyers her head spun, but opinion had all been with Kass. She could never return to Alp de Ciel. She had no rights at all.

She'd lost her son.

Finally, when the fuss had died—when the press had stopped looking for her—she'd returned to Australia. She'd applied for the job here under her mother's maiden name.

She'd never touched a cent of royal money. She'd rather have died.

And now here he was. Her son. Five years old and she knew nothing of him.

And Matty? What had he been told of his mother?

'What do you know about me?' she asked the little boy, while the big man with the gentle eyes looked at her with sympathy.

'My father said you were a whore,' Matty said matter-of-factly as he carried over the plates, obviously not knowing what the word meant. 'But Aunt Laura and Uncle Rafael have now told me that you're a nice lady who digs old things out of the ground and finds out about the people who owned them. Aunt Laura says that you're an arch...an archaeologist.'

'I am,' she said softly, wonderingly.

'My mother and I have told Matty as much of the truth as we know,' Rafael told her. The cake plates were in front of them now, and they were seated round the table almost like a family. The fire crackled in the old wood-stove. The rain pattered on the roof outside and the whole scene was so domestic it made Kelly feel she'd been picked up and transported to another world.

'Kellyn, my mother and I would like you to return,' Rafael said, so gently that she blinked. Her weird little bubble burst and she couldn't catch hold of the fragments.

'Return?'

'To Alp de Ciel.'

'You have to be kidding.' But she couldn't take her eyes from Matty.

'Mathieu is Crown Prince of Alp de Ciel.'

She couldn't take this in. 'I…I guess.'

'I'm Prince Regent until he comes of age.'

'Congratulations.' It sounded absurd. Nothing in life had prepared her for this. Matty was calmly sitting across the table eating chocolate cake, watching her closely with wide brown eyes that were…hers, she thought, suddenly fighting an almost irresistible urge to laugh. Hysteria was very, very close.

Matty was watching her as she was watching him. Maybe…maybe he even wanted a mother. He wanted her?

This was her baby. She longed with every fibre of her being to take him in her arms and hug him as she'd dreamed of holding him for these last five years. But this was a self-contained little person who'd been brought up in circumstances of which she knew nothing. To have an unknown woman—even if it had been explained who she was—hugging and sobbing, she knew instinctively it would drive him away.

'I'll never go back to Alp de Ciel,' she whispered but she knew it was a lie the moment she said it. She'd left the little principality shattered. To go back… To go back to her son… Her little son who was looking at her with equal amounts of hope and fear?

'It would be very different now,' Rafael said. 'You'd be returning as the mother of the Crown Prince. You'd be accepted in all honour.'

'You know what was said of me?'

'Kass said it over and over, of all his women,' Rafael said. 'The people stopped believing Kass a long time ago.'

'Kass was Matty's father,' she said with an urgent glance at Matty, but Rafael shook his head.

'Matty hardly knew his father. Matty, can you remember the last time you saw Prince Kass?'

'At Christmas?' Matty said, sounding doubtful. 'With the lady in the really pointy shoes. I saw his picture in the paper when he was dead. Aunt Laura said we should feel sad so I did. May I have some more chocolate cake, please? It's very good.'

'Certainly you can,' Kelly whispered. 'But Kass…Kass said he intended to raise him himself.'

'Kass intended nothing but his own pleasure,'

Rafael said roughly. 'The people knew that. There's little regret at the accident that killed him.'

'Oh, Matty,' Kelly whispered, and the little boy looked up at her and calmly met her gaze.

'Ellen and Marguerite say I should still be sad because my papa is dead,' he said. 'But it's very hard to stay sad. My tortoise, Hermione, died at Christmas. I was very sad when Hermione died so when I think of Papa I try and think of Hermione.'

'Who are Ellen and Marguerite?'

'They're my friends. Ellen makes my bed and cleans my room. Marguerite takes me for walks. Marguerite is married to Tony who works in the garden. Tony gives me rides in his wheelbarrow. He helped me to bury Hermione and we planted a rhod…a rhododendron on top of her.'

He went back to cutting cake. Rafael watched her for a while as she watched her son.

'So you're in charge?' she managed at last.

'Unfortunately, yes.'

'Unfortunately?'

She gazed across the table at his hands. They were big and strong and work-stained. Vaguely she remembered Kass's hands. A prince's hands. Long and lean and smooth as silk.

Rafael's thumb was missing half a nail and

was carrying the remains of an angry, green-purple bruise.

'What do you do for a living?' she asked. 'When…when you're not a Prince Regent.'

'I invent toys. And make 'em.'

It was so out of left field that she blinked.

'Toys?'

'I design them from the ground up,' he said, sounding cheerful for a moment. 'My company distributes worldwide.'

'Uncle Rafael makes Robo-Craft,' Matty volunteered with such pride in his voice that Kelly knew this was a very important part of her small son's world.

'Robo-Craft,' she repeated, and even Kelly, cloistered away in her historical world, was impressed. She knew it.

Robo-Craft was a construction kit, where each part except the motor was crafted individually in wood. One could give a set of ten pieces to a four-year-old, plus the tiny mechanism that went with it, and watch the child achieve a construction that worked. It could be a tiny carousel if the blocks were placed above the mechanism, or a weird creature that moved in crazy ways if the mechanism was in contact with the floor. The motor was absurdly strong, so inventions could be as big as desired. As kids grew older they could expand their sets to make wonderful inventions of their own, fashioning their own pieces to fit. Robo-Craft had been written up as a return to the tool-shed, encouraging boys and girls alike to attack plywood with handsaws and paint.

'They say it encourages kids to be kids again,' Kelly whispered, awed. 'Like building cubby houses.'

'Uncle Rafael helped me build a cubby house in the palace garden,' Matty volunteered. 'We did it just before we left.'

'So you do spend time in the castle?' she asked him. She was finding it so hard to look at anything that wasn't Matty, yet Rafael's presence was somehow…intriguing? Unable to be ignored.

'I've been there since Kass died.'

'But not before.'

'My mother still lives in the dower house. I didn't see eye to eye with Kass or his father and left the country as soon as I was able, but my mother…well, the memories of her life there with my father are a pretty strong hold. And then there's Matty. She loves him.'

So it seemed that at least her little son had been

loved. Her nightmares of the last five years had been impersonal nannies, paid carers, no love at all. But thanks to this man's mother… And now thanks to this man…

'What do I do now?' Kelly whispered, and Rafael looked at her with sympathy.

'Get to know your son.'

'But…why?'

'Kelly, my mother and I have talked this through. Yes, Matty's the Crown Prince of Alp de Ciel, but you're his mother. What happens now is up to you. Even if you insist he stay here until he's of an age to make up his mind…no matter what the lawyers say, we've decided it's your right to make that decision. You're his mother again, Kellyn. Starting now.'

CHAPTER TWO

To say Kelly was stunned would be an understatement. She was blown away. For five years she had dreamed of this moment—of this time when she'd be with her son again. But she'd never imagined it could be like this.

It was ordinary. Domestic. World-shattering.

'Why don't you take a bath and get some dry clothes on?' Rafael suggested, and the move between world-shattering and ordinary seemed almost shocking.

'Excuse me?'

'You're wet through,' he said. 'You've been shivering since we met you, and it's not just shock. You've been ill. You shouldn't stay wet. Matty and I aren't going anywhere. We'll stay here and eat your chocolate cake and wait for you.'

'But…where are you staying?'

'We have a place booked in town,' he said. 'But there are things we need to discuss before we leave. Go take your bath and we'll talk afterwards.'

She had no choice but to agree. Her head wasn't working for her. If he'd told her to walk the plank she might calmly have done it right now.

And she couldn't stop shivering.

So she left them and ran a bath, thinking she'd dip in and out and return to them fast. But when she sank into the hot water her body reacted with a weird lethargy that kept her right where she was.

She had no shower—just this lovely deep bath tub. The water pressure was great, which meant that by the time she'd fumbled through getting her clothes off the bath was filled. The water enveloped her, cocooned her, deepening the trance-like state she'd felt ever since she'd seen Matty.

She could hear them talking through the door.

'She makes very good cake.' That was Matty. As a compliment it was just about the loveliest thing she could imagine. Her grandmother had given her the chocolate cake recipe. Her son was eating her grandma's chocolate cake.

'I think your mama is a very clever lady.' That was Rafael. His compliment didn't give her the same kind of tingle. She thought of the lovely things Kass had said to her when he'd wanted to marry her, and she still cringed that she'd believed him. This man was a de Boutaine. Every sense in her body was screaming *beware*.

'Why is she clever?' Matty asked.

'She's an archaeologist and a historian. Archaeologists need to be clever.'

'Why?'

'They have to figure out…how old things are. Stuff like that.'

'Was that why she was at our castle? Trying to figure out how old it is?'

'I guess.'

'It's five hundred and sixty-three years old,' Matty said. 'Crater told me. It's in a book. Mama could have just read the book.'

'People like your mama would have written the book. She could have worked it out. Maybe you could ask her how.'

'She does make good cake,' Matty said and Kelly slid deeper into the hot water and felt as if she'd died and gone to heaven.

What did they want? Where would she take things from here? No matter. For this moment nothing mattered but that her son was sitting by her kitchen fire eating her grandma's cake.

* * *

She hadn't taken dry clothes into the bathroom. This was a tiny cottage and her bathroom led straight off the kitchen. She hadn't been thinking, and once she was scrubbed dry, pinkly warm, wrapped in her big, fuzzy bathrobe and matching pink slippers she kept in the bathroom permanently and with her hair wrapped in a towel, she felt absurdly self-conscious about facing them again.

There was hardly a back route from bathroom to bedroom unless she dived out of the window. Face them she must, so she opened the door and they both turned and smiled.

They'd been setting the table. There were plates and spoons and knives in three settings. Rafael had cut the bread on the sideboard. The sense of domesticity was almost overwhelming.

'That's much better,' he said approvingly, his dark eyes checking her from the fluffy slippers up.

'You look pretty,' Matty said and then amended his statement. 'Comfy pretty. Not like the ladies my papa brought to the castle.'

She flushed.

'You're pink,' Matty said, and she flushed some more.

'I guess the water was too hot.'

'At least you're warm,' Rafael said. 'Sit down and eat. I know we've done this the wrong way round—cake before soup—but it does seem sensible to eat. That is, if you don't mind sharing.'

'I…no, of course I don't mind. But it's all I've got.'

'Until next pay day?' he asked, teasing, and she flushed even more. Drat her stupid habit of blushing. Though, come to think of it, she hadn't blushed for a very long time.

'I meant soup and toast is all there is.'

'After a hard day down the gold-mines? It's hardly workman's fare.'

'I need to get dressed,' she said.

'You're not hungry?'

She was hungry. She'd fiddled with her cake, not able to pay it any attention. Now she was suddenly aware that she was ravenous.

But to sit in her bathrobe…

'We're jet lagged,' Rafael said, seeing her indecision. 'We need to get some sleep pretty soon, but this soup smells so good we'd love to share. If you don't mind eating now.'

She gave up. Thinking was just too hard. 'Fine.'

'Great,' he said.

'We can't find your toaster,' Matty told her, moving right on to important matters.

'I make my toast with the fire.'

'How?'

Okay. She was dressed in a bathrobe and fluffy slippers and nothing else. She was entertaining the Prince Regent and the Crown Prince of Alp de Ciel in her kitchen. A girl just had to gather her wits and teach them how to make toast.

She tied another knot—firmly—in the front of her bathrobe, flipped open the fire door and produced a toasting fork. She pulled a chair up to the stove, lifted Matty on to it—she couldn't believe she did that—she just lifted him on to the chair as if it were the most natural thing in the world—she arranged a piece of bread on the toasting fork and set him to work.

It was the first time she'd touched him. She felt breathless.

'Wow,' Matty breathed and she smiled, and Matty turned to see if Rafael was smiling too, and so did Kelly and suddenly she didn't feel like breathing.

It was the shock, she told herself. Not the smile. Not.

It was his cousin's smile. The de Boutaine smile.

She remembered almost every detail of Kass's courtship. One moment she'd been part of a team excavating in the palace grounds; the next she'd looked up and Kass had been watching her. He had been on his great, black stallion.

He'd been just what a prince ought to look like—tall and dark and heart-stoppingly handsome, with a dangerous glint behind his stunning smile. And his horse… She'd spent half her childhood with thoroughbreds but the stallion had made her gasp. The combination, prince and stallion, had been enough to change her world.

'Cinderella,' he murmured. 'Just who I need.'

It was a strange comment, but then he left his horse, stooped beside her in the dust and watched her brush the dust from an ancient pipeline she was uncovering. He seemed truly interested. He spent an hour watching her and then he asked her out to dinner.

'Anywhere your heart desires,' he told her. 'This Principality is yours to command.'

He meant it was his to command. Kass's ego was the size of his country, but it had taken her too long to find that out.

Stunned, she went out to dinner with him. She was mesmerized by his looks, his charm and the fact that he seemed equally fascinated by her. It was heady stuff.

The next morning he met her at the stables. He mounted her on a mare, almost as beautiful as his stallion, Blaze, and they rode together into the foothills of the mountains in the early morning mist. The magic of the morning blew her away. It left her feeling mind-numbingly, blissfully in love, transported to a parallel universe where normal rules of sense and caution no longer applied.

That night, as she finished work, he appeared again, in his dress uniform. Regal and imperious and still utterly charming, he was focusing all his attention on her. He'd just come from a ceremonial function, he told her, but she suspected now that he'd dressed that way to overwhelm her.

And overwhelmed she was. Royalty and stallions. Swords and braid and wealth. He chartered a private plane to take her to Paris. No matter that she had nothing to wear—they'd shop for clothes in Fabourg Saint-Honoré, he told her. He'd take her personally this night, before their weekend started.

For Kelly, the only child of disinterested academic parents, whose only love had been her neighbour's horses, this seemed a fairy-tale.

Instead it was a nightmare. One where she ended up losing everything.

So now Rafael was smiling at her and there was no way she was smiling back. That way led to disaster. Royalty…no and no and no.

'I'm not Kass,' he said and she blinked.

'Pardon?'

'I know there's a family resemblance,' he told her, and there was a note of anger behind his studied gentleness. 'But I'm not Kass and I'm not like him. You have no reason to fear me, Kelly.'

'I…'

'Let's make toast,' he said, and smiled some more and supervised turning the bread on the toasting fork. 'You pour the soup.'

So eat they did, by the fireside. Matty was hungry and Kelly was hungry for him. She could scarcely take her eyes from him.

'He'll still be here tomorrow,' Rafael said and leaned over the table, filled her soup spoon and guided her lifeless hand to her lips. 'You look like you need a feed as much as Matty.'

'You'll still be here tomorrow?'

'Yes.'

There should have been a fuss, she thought,

bewildered. She thought of Kass, flying to Paris that first weekend she'd met him. There'd been minions everywhere—pomp and pageantry, recognition of Kass's rank and dignity.

'Why aren't there reporters?' she asked, forcing herself to drink her soup as Rafael had directed, if only to stop him force-feeding her. He had the look of a man who just might.

He was frowning at her. He looked as if he was worried about her. That was crazy.

'Just how sick were you?' he demanded and she flushed and spooned a bit more soup in.

'It was a horrid flu but I'm fine now. You haven't answered my question. Why are there no reporters? If you're indeed Prince Regent…'

'We came incognito.'

'Oh, sure.'

'It can be done,' he said. 'In fact I changed my name to my mother's when I left the country. I have an American passport—I'm Rafael Nadine.'

'And Matty?'

'Trickier,' he said. 'But not impossible when you know people in high places.'

'As you do.'

'As we do,' he said gravely. 'It was important. To sweep in here in a Rolls-Royce or six with a royal entourage behind me…it wouldn't achieve what I hoped to achieve.'

'Which was what?'

'To find out for sure what my investigators have been telling me. That you are indeed a woman of principle. That you are indeed a woman who should have all the access to your son that you want.'

'Oh,' she said faintly.

'Eat your soup.'

'I don't think…'

'We're not talking about anything else until you've eaten your soup and at least three slices of toast,' he said roughly. 'Matty, something tells me your mama needs a little looking after. As a son, that's your duty. Finish your soup and then make us all some more toast.'

Matty crashed. Just like that. One minute he was bright and bubbly and enthused about toast-making, but the next minute, as he ate his third piece of toast, spread thickly with honey, his eyelids drooped. He pushed aside his plate, put his head on his hands and sighed.

'My head feels heavy,' he said. 'Uncle Rafael…'

'We need to go,' Rafael said ruefully. 'We

hadn't meant to stay this long.' He smiled at her—that damned smile again. 'It's your fault. The soup smelled so good.'

'Where are you staying?' she asked.

'The Prince Edward.'

'But that's…' She paused, dismayed.

'That's what?' Rafael said. 'We found it on the Internet, Matty and I. It looks splendid. We checked in this afternoon and it seems really comfortable.'

'Yes, but it's over a really popular pub,' she said. 'Thursday night here is most people's pay night. The Prince Edward is the party pub. By two in the morning it'll be moving up and down on its foundations.'

'Oh,' he said, in a voice which said that if Matty hadn't been present he might have said something else.

'I need to go to sleep,' Matty said unnecessarily.

'You can stay here,' Kelly said before she realized she intended to say it.

'We can't…'

'I've just got the one bedroom,' she said quickly. 'But it's a double bed. You and Matty could have it and I can sleep on the settee.'

'This settee?' Rafael asked. There was no

separate living area from the kitchen in this cottage. The settee stretched out along one wall, big and piled with cushions and incredibly inviting.

'I could sleep on that,' Matty announced.

'So you could,' Rafael said. 'If that's okay with your mama. I'll go back to the Prince Edward.'

Matty's face fell. 'I want to go with you,' he whispered.

Of course. Kelly was his mother but he'd known her for all of two hours. Rafael was his security.

But now she'd said it, Kelly knew the invitation had come from the heart. She so wanted them to stay. She wanted *Matty* to stay.

Rafael was watching her face. He wouldn't have to be brilliant to see the aching need she had no way of disguising.

The thought of them going to the Prince Edward, where she knew they'd lie awake all night rocked by the vibrations of truly appalling bands was almost unbearable. But in truth the thought of Matty going anywhere was unbearable. She'd put up with Rafael—with a de Boutaine in her house—to know that Matty was under her roof.

'So here's a plan,' Rafael said gently, looking from Matty to Kelly and back again. 'Matty, your mama says the hotel we're planning on staying in is very noisy. She's invited us to stay in this little cottage with her. Would you like to do that?'

'Yes, but only if you stay here too,' Matty said, and his bottom lip trembled.

'Then I will,' Rafael said. 'But you know, you and your mama look as tired as each other. Why don't you pop under the blankets on one side of your mama's bed? Your mama can sleep on the other side and I'll sleep by the fire.'

'Why can't you and mama sleep in the bed while I sleep by the fire?' Matty whispered but he was losing force. He was drooping as they watched.

'It wouldn't be dignified,' Rafael said. 'You know Aunt Laura says you and I need to learn to be dignified.'

'It's not dignified to sleep in the same bed as my mama?'

'For you, yes. For me, no.'

'Okay,' Matty said, caving in with an alacrity born of need. 'Can I go to bed now?'

And an hour later she was in bed with her son.

It felt like a weird and spacey dream. She lay in her big double bed and listened to him. Her son was breathing.

No big deal. To listen to a child breathe…

How could she go to sleep? She'd left the blind open and the moon was shining over her little vegetable garden, into the window, washing over her little son's face.

Normally she blocked the moon out. She had a single woman's need for security—privacy— so the blind went down every night.

There was no way the blind was coming down this night. She lay and watched Matty's chest rise and fall, his small face intent even in sleep, the way his lashes curled, the way his fingers pressed into his cheek…

She could see his father. She could see the de Boutaine side. But she could also see little things about herself. She had funny quirky eyebrows, too thick for beauty. Whenever she had a haircut, the hairdresser tut-tutted and thinned them out.

Here were those same thick brows.

On a guy they'd be gorgeous.

On Matty they were gorgeous.

Her son.

There were vague sounds from outside and she looked out of the window in time to see the security guards wandering past her back fence.

Yes, she should get up and close the blind. It wasn't safe.

It was safe, for just through the door Rafael de Boutaine was stretched out on her settee.

Her son was in bed beside her. The Prince Regent of Alp de Ciel was just through the door.

'As if that makes us safe,' she muttered into the night.

But…but…

'He's different from Kass. He's honourable, I know.

'How do you know?' She was whispering into the dark. Her hand was lying on Matty's pillow. She wouldn't touch him. She wouldn't for the world wake him, startle him. But with her hand on his pillow she could feel his breathing. It was enough.

'Rafael brought him home.

'There must be some underlying motive.

'Maybe, but he's brought him home,' she whispered and the thought of Rafael lying in the darkness just through the door remained solid. Good. Comforting in a way she hadn't been comforted for years.

Her little boy was asleep beside her. Rafael had brought him to her.

What more could a woman want?

'I have my son,' she whispered into the dark and thought how could she sleep with such happiness?

But she was still recuperating from the flu. She hadn't slept well for weeks.

She leaned up on her elbows and gazed for one long last moment at her son. She touched her lips with her finger and then transferred the kiss to her son with a feather touch that wouldn't disturb him for the world.

She snuggled down on to her pillows where she could watch her son's breathing.

He breathed. He breathed.

Rafael was just through the door. Prince Regent of Alp de Ciel. A prince who'd brought her son to her.

She felt warm and safe and almost delirious with love.

She slept.

Kelly woke to the smell of coffee. She opened one eye. They were standing at the bedroom door, smiling. Both of them. Identical smiles, where warmth and mischief combined.

Rafael was dressed in the same casual cords and soft sweater he'd been wearing the night before.

Last night Matty had been wearing jeans and a soft blue coat. Now he was wearing almost identical cords to Rafael and a sweater of the same colour as well. They looked… They looked…

She blinked fiercely. She'd been awake for seconds and she was close to tears already.

'H…hi.'

'Hi, yourself, sleepyhead,' Rafael said, carrying in a mug of steaming coffee. 'Mathieu. Toast.' Mathieu almost saluted, but his hands were occupied in balancing a plateful of toast.

The toast was spread liberally with marmalade and butter. Yum. But…

She glanced at the bedside clock and sat bolt upright as Matty reached the bed with the toast. It was almost a calamity, but not quite, for Rafael moved like a big cat, pouncing on the plate, lifting it away while spilling not a drop of coffee.

She was stunned, but she was still staring at the clock. 'It's after nine,' she stammered. 'How…'

'We turned off your alarm clock,' Matty said proudly and removed the plate of toast from Rafael's grasp and put it carefully on her knee. 'Uncle Rafael and me woke up really early because it doesn't feel like morning. Uncle Rafael says it's because we're all the way round the other side of the world and the sun hasn't caught us up. Uncle Rafael says if we keep flying we'll catch up with it again but we don't want to keep flying yet 'cos we have to give you toast. And the man outside in the uniform said you've been really, really sick and someone ought to look after you 'cos you sure as hell don't look after yourself.'

He paused, looking up at Rafael with uncertainty. 'Did I say that right? In *Anglais*?'

'You certainly did,' Rafael said. 'I told you my mother's American,' he told Kelly. 'Matty's been brought up bilingual. Isn't he terrific?'

'Terrific,' Kelly said and managed a smile. Terrific? He was more than terrific. He was... he was...

Her son.

But there was still the little matter of the time.

'I'm supposed to be at work.'

'You're not. Rob's back,' Rafael said. 'The two tour guides are back at work today. There's no urgency. The powers that be say you're to take the day off if you need.'

'The powers that be...'

'We've been busy,' he told her. 'We went back to the hotel to get our gear. Then we visited your administration. The lady there—Diane?—she was in at eight. We introduced ourselves.'

'You never told her…'

'We said we were relations,' he said, placating her. 'And we were worried about you. It seems Diane is worried about you too.'

'She's a mother hen,' Kelly said fretfully, wondering what Diane would be thinking. Knowing what Diane would be thinking. 'Look, thank you for the thought but I need to…'

'Take us through the theme park,' Rafael said. 'Matty's aching to go down a gold-mine. We thought we might do that first, if it's okay with you.' He smiled down at her with that heart-stopping smile that sent her brain straight into panic. 'That is, unless you'd like to stay in bed and sleep while Matty and I explore?'

Matty explore without her? The idea had her reaching to toss off her covers but Rafael caught her hands and stopped her.

'No,' he said, gently but firmly. 'You stay in bed until you've had your toast. Matty and I are going to eat more toast until you're ready. You're not to rush. We have all the time in the world.'

'Really?'

The smile faded. 'No,' he admitted. 'Not really.

But for today I'm going to pretend that's true, so I'd like you to play along if you will. Let's get ourselves breakfasted and go find some gold.'

She wore her favourite dress. Matty's words stayed with her—*I thought my mother would wear a pretty dress.* So she did.

Most of Kelly's work in the theme park was done in the administration. She researched new displays, she assessed the veracity of potential tenants for the commercial sites—were their wares truly representative of the eighteen-fifties? She worked with the engineers as they combined authentic mining methods with new-age safety. She examined artefacts as they were found, donated or offered for sale.

In the short times she was off site she wore what the park staff loosely termed civvies, but while she was in the park, like every other employee, she dressed for the times.

She loved her clothes. Yes, she had the hard-wearing moleskins and flannels for when she needed to go underground, but mostly she was a woman wearing clothes that a woman would have worn in the eighteen-fifties—hooped skirts, shawls, bonnets. She loved the way her skirts swished against her, how they turned her into a citizen of a bygone age. She loved disappearing into the world of nearly two hundred years ago.

And this morning Matty was waiting for his mother. So she chose a pale blue muslin gown, beautifully hand-embroidered herself in the long winter nights before the fire. She teamed it with a soft woollen shawl of a deeper blue and cream. She tied her soft chestnut curls into a knot and placed a bonnet on top, a soft straw confection with ribbons of three colours combined. Then she pinched her cheeks to give them colour as girls used to do in times past. She smiled to herself. She was dressing for her son. Surely he wouldn't notice colour in her cheeks.

She was also dressing for Rafael and he might.

Which was a nonsense, she told herself, suddenly angry. She wasn't dressing for Rafael. She'd never dress for a de Boutaine again. She wanted nothing to do with the family.

But her son was a de Boutaine. How could she swear never to have anything to do with a royal family headed by her son?

It was too hard. It made her head spin. She picked up the little cane basket she carried instead of a purse and opened the door to the kitchen.

They were washing dishes. Rafael was washing, Matty was wiping. Rafael had his sleeves rolled up. He'd used too much soap and suds were oozing out of the porcelain bowl and on to the wooden bench. Matty was manfully trying to wipe suds off plates. He had suds on his nose.

There it was again. The combination of de Boutaine sexiness that made her want to gasp.

She swallowed it firmly, but both guys had turned to her and were looking at her in frank admiration.

'Wow,' said Matty.

'Wow,' Rafael repeated and she felt herself blushing.

'I…it's what we all have to wear.'

'My mama's pretty,' Matty said, satisfied. 'Isn't she, Uncle Rafael?'

'She certainly is,' Rafael agreed. 'Modern men don't know what they're missing.'

'It certainly covers me,' she said, struggling for lightness. 'There could be absolutely anything under these hoops.'

'Hoops,' Matty said. He walked forward, fascinated, and gave one of her hoops a tentative poke.

Her skirt swayed out behind her.

'It's like a little tent,' Matty said. 'Mama could

have really, really fat legs. Or she could be hiding something. A little dog.'

It was said with a certain amount of hope and for a dumb moment Kelly wished she had a dog.

A dog under her skirt. Right.

'There's nothing your mama needs to hide,' Rafael said, turning his back to the suds, eyeing them with a degree of bewilderment and then sternly turning back to her. 'Let's go play on the goldfields.'

'You haven't finished washing up.'

'My suds seem to be taking over the world,' he said. 'I just shook the little holder with the washing up liquid in and suds went everywhere. I think we should go out and shut the door and lock it after us. And hope like crazy the suds don't follow us down the mineshafts.'

They loved it.

Kelly could do the guide thing on autopilot. She walked them through the little town, down to the creek where tourists were panning for gold. She showed the boys how to use the tin pans and then sat on a log and watched them.

The park was quiet. The flu epidemic had hit the whole state. It was autumn. Nearly all the staff had been laid low early and were now returning to work. With the worst of the sickness past, they'd be almost overmanned for the rest of the season. So she could afford to take this day. To simply watch as Matty and Rafael explored.

They were so alike.

Rafael wasn't even Matty's uncle, she reminded herself. Rafael had been Kass's cousin. That made him—what—second cousin to Matty?

But Matty loved him. He trusted him absolutely. Their two heads were bowed over the pan, searching for specks of gold, and she thought that Rafael could easily be his father.

What sort of man was he? The Prince Regent of Alp de Ciel.

It didn't matter.

It did matter, for there was a burning question hanging over her head. Where did she go from here?

She'd been handed back her son, but Matty was his own little person. He had allegiances. There were people he loved, and those people didn't include her.

Rafael had said it was her decision to make.

She'd keep him here. She watched as he found a tiny speck of gold in his pan and held it on his thumb, admiring. He could live with her here. She'd take care of him. He could have a wonderful life, living on the diggings. Lots of staff had their kids here—he'd be part of the kid-pack who wore period clothes and treated the park as their personal playground. He'd go to school here. She'd keep him…

Hidden?

It was on the tip of her tongue, the edge of her thoughts. That was what she'd been doing, she thought. For the last five years she'd been hiding. She was hiding still, behind her hoops and her bonnet and her period self.

The Kelly who'd looked up to see Prince Kass gazing down at her, the Kelly who'd ridden out with Kass at dawn, who'd launched herself into life six years back, had been locked firmly away.

Yes, she was hiding. She was still in there somewhere, the Kelly who craved excitement and adventure and…romance? But she was very firmly hidden and there was no way the sensible Kelly would ever let her emerge again.

Pete was walking down the hill towards them. Trouble. She knew the security guard well and the expression on his face had Kelly standing up, moving automatically between Pete and the two gold-panners.

Between the outside world and her son.

'What's wrong?' she called before he reached her, and Rafael looked up from gold-panning, handed the pan over to Matty and came to join her.

'There's media at the gate,' Pete said harshly. 'They're asking Diane where to find someone called the Prince Regent of some country or other. Diane told them she's never heard of anyone like that but they described—' he hesitated as Rafael reached them '—they described you, sir.'

'Damn,' Rafael said, but he said it wearily as if he'd expected it.

'We'll go back to the cottage,' Kelly said, uncertain, but he shook his head.

'They'd find us there. We'll be forced to stay inside while they camp and wait for us to come out. It'll just delay the inevitable.'

'I can see them off,' Pete said. 'Begging your pardon, but… are you a prince?'

'For my sins, yes,' Rafael said ruefully. 'And this is a public theme park. They can demand admission. I'll have to head them off. Kelly, can you blend into the tourist scene with Matty?'

'I…sure. Are they looking for me?' She

sounded scared. She knew it but there wasn't anything she could do about it. Five years ago she'd been hunted as the press had searched the world for her. She'd been turned into the wicked princess, reviled by all.

To have photographers here now…

'Not yet,' Rafael said. 'At least I hope not. I hope it's just that they've tracked me down. They'll assume Matty's at home in Alp de Ciel.'

'What have you told them? Do they know you're letting me have access to Matty?'

'I've told them nothing,' he said, looking grim. 'But it's not going to last.'

'What's going on?' Pete demanded, bewildered.

'It's private,' Kelly said urgently, but she knew Pete's brain was forming questions more quickly than his mouth could ask them.

'They'll find us soon,' she whispered.

'Yes, but I'll buy time.' Rafael shrugged. 'I'm sorry, Matty,' he said. Matty had straightened from his panning and was looking bewildered. 'It's the press,' he said, as if that explained all, and Kelly could see that the words were meaningful to her little son. He'd been hounded by the media in the past, then. 'I need to go.'

'Will I come with you?' Matty drew himself up

and Kelly had a flash of recognition. This was a prince in training. His shoulders came back and he met Rafael's look directly. 'Do they wish to talk to me?'

'They might eventually,' Rafael conceded. 'But your job here is to protect your mother. If it's okay,' he said to Kelly, 'I'll leave—I'll give them some sort of interview and try to deflect them—and come back when the park is closed. Matty, is that okay with you?'

'Y-yes,' Matty said but his bottom lip trembled again. He really was a very little boy.

'We'll have fun,' Kelly said, stooping to look directly into his eyes. 'Matty, we can go down a gold-mine. We can play tenpin bowling with old wooden skittles. Do you know how to bowl?'

'Y-yes.'

'We can learn how to make damper—it's a lovely type of bread that's really Australian. Then we can go back to my little house and sit by the fire and read books. Before you know it, your Uncle Rafael will be back.'

'I want my Aunt Laura,' Matty quavered, and Kelly couldn't help herself. She gathered him to her and hugged. His little body was stiff and unyielding.

'They're coming this way,' Pete said urgently and Rafael looked up the hill and swore.

'Damn, I…'

'Just go,' Kelly said, holding Matty tight. 'Please.' She wasn't ready to face the media yet and the thought of cameras aimed at Matty was unbearable. 'But you will come back?'

'Of course I'll come back.'

'Thank you,' she said simply and, as Pete moved up the hill to deflect the dozen or so men and women walking purposefully towards them, she crossed the little bridge over the creek and carried Matty away. Hoping the media had been too far away to guess that she and Rafael had been together.

The Chinese camp was just behind them. Yan, the camp guide, was a personal friend.

'Can I take Matty through the Joss house?' she demanded and Yan stepped aside. The inside of the Joss house was a sacred place, out of bounds for anyone but worshippers.

'Go,' he said without asking questions, his eyes flicking to the group of men and women clustering about Rafael. Shouting questions. Lifting cameras high and taking photographs over people's heads.

She went. But before Yan closed the gate behind her she turned with Matty in her arms to take a last glimpse of Rafael.

Royalty.

She wanted no part of it.

She had a part of it. He was in her arms right now, tense and frightened and to be protected at all costs.

Her Matty. Her son.

The only person standing between Matty and the media—between Matty and the world—was Rafael.

A de Boutaine.

Her world was upside down.

'Let's go underground for a while,' she whispered to Matty as she fled out through the back entrance.

'I don't think I want to go underground,' Matty said and Kelly thought, neither do I.

She'd had five years of being underground.

Maybe it was time to emerge.

Maybe she had no choice.

CHAPTER THREE

THEY explored the goldfields until Matty's legs gave out. He was cheerful, interested and polite. They ate their dinner early—a damper they'd made together and a thick Irish stew. Kelly settled him into her big bed and his eyelids drooped.

Fatigue was sapping his courage. He was half a world away from his people.

'I want Uncle Rafael,' he murmured.

'He'll come,' Kelly said. 'But he said he might not be able to return until late. I'll have him come in here and say goodnight the minute he arrives.'

'Do you promise?'

'I promise.'

'I miss Aunt Laura,' he said fretfully. 'I miss Ellen and Marguerite. I want to go home.'

Her heart twisted. Home. Home was where the heart was.

Her home was right here. Her home was with this small boy, who was so alone.

The Crown Prince of Alp de Ciel.

'Let me read you a story,' she said, and she found an ancient book she'd loved when she had been his age, a book she'd held on to just in case, just in case...

The Poky Little Puppy.

The book was battered and dog-eared. It had been given to her by her grandmother when she had been just Matty's age. She'd loved it.

So did Matty. He relaxed, snuggling into his pillows. She so wanted to lift him into her arms, to cuddle him to sleep, but she knew he wasn't ready for that. She was a stranger even if she was his mother.

She had to get to know him slowly.

Could he stay on the diggings with her?

'My Aunt Laura will like this story,' Matty murmured sleepily. 'Can you read it to Uncle Rafael when he comes?'

'I...yes.'

He had his own people. His own family.

Where did she fit in?

She didn't know.

He came at nine p.m., after she'd almost given up on him. She'd expected a call from security at the gate, but instead there was a soft knock on the door.

She opened it and there he was.

But it wasn't the Rafael she'd seen before. This was… This was…

His Royal Highness, Prince Rafael, Prince Regent of Alp de Ciel. He was wearing full dress regalia. A deep blue-black suit, immaculately cut. A slash of gold across his chest. Rows of medals and insignia at his breast and a dress sword at his side.

She took an instinctive step back. Kass…

'Gorgeous, aren't I?' he said and any resemblance to Kass flew out of the window. Kass, laughing at himself? No way.

'I…yes. Very pretty,' she managed and he grinned.

'Can I come in?'

'Where's the rest of the royal entourage?'

'I gave them the slip,' Rafael said. 'You have no idea how much trouble I had getting back here.'

'Maybe jeans and a windcheater might be more appropriate for creeping round after dark.'

'Yes, but I wouldn't have had my sword for coping with bogeymen.' He grimaced down at his gorgeous self. 'Don't worry, Kelly. I hate this as much as you do. Politics demanded that I bring it, however, and politics demand that I talk to you now. Can I come in?'

She stood wordlessly aside as he walked in, hauled his jacket off, unbuttoned the top three buttons of his stiffly starched shirt and set his sword by the door.

Royalty off duty.

'So you thought you might change into dress uniform… why?' she asked faintly as he opened the fire box on the stove and held his hands out for warmth.

'Press conference and hastily organised civil reception,' he said briefly. 'With your mayor. You can't imagine how excited everyone is.'

'Um…why?'

'Alp de Ciel is known for its gold-mining,' he said blandly. 'We've heard that this is the best theme park in the world for showcasing historical events. What could be more natural than the Prince Regent of Alp de Ciel—needing a little breathing-space from the demands of his royal duties—doing a little exploring?'

'They never believed it.'

'They did,' he said. 'The press believe what they want to believe. This makes a fabulous story. Prince found incognito in local theme park. Prince agrees to have dinner with local bigwigs for photographic opportunity. Prince excuses himself towards the end of dinner pleading jet lag but everyone's got their photographs by now. So I slipped away.'

'You had your dress uniform with you just on the off chance of a photographic opportunity?'

His smile faded. 'I did suspect,' he said, 'that this journey might be discovered. Like it or not, I'm now head of state of Alp de Ciel. For me to come to Australia and not give a press conference at least would be an insult. The palace officials told me that in no uncertain terms. So yes, I brought my royal toggery. No, I didn't want to unpack it but here it is, in all its glory.'

She was staring at the medals, fascinated.

'So tonight,' she said. 'You just…slipped away from your royal reception. You called a cab—wearing that?'

'Yes, it was hard giving everyone the slip but the limousine driver's currently miffed because I took a cab and a cab driver's happily pocketed a fare and a half for dropping me in the middle of nowhere and saying nothing. It was only a mile or so down the road and I kept to the shadows.'

'Wearing your dress sword.' She couldn't keep her eyes off his chest. It was some…chest.

'A prince has to be prepared,' he said patiently. 'In case of bogeymen.' His smile deepened. 'Stop looking like that. Pete let me in and he's under instructions to say no one's come. He'll admit no one else.'

She shook her head in disbelief. 'You think you're clever,' she said wonderingly.

'I do,' he said smugly.

'Matty wants you to wake him and say goodnight.'

His face stilled. 'He was okay with you?'

'Yes.'

'But he was asking for me?'

'He loves you. You and your mother.'

'I guess that hurts,' he said cautiously.

'I can't expect anything else.'

'He'll learn…'

'I don't think he can stay here,' she whispered and something in her face had him crossing the room to her in two swift strides and taking her hands in his.

'Kelly, don't look like that.'

'Like…like what?'

'As if you're tearing yourself in two.'

'I'm not. I'm not. Go and say goodnight to Matty.' She pulled away from him roughly. For a moment he stood, looking down at her face, obviously troubled, but she wouldn't look at him.

Finally he wheeled away. He disappeared into the bedroom. She stood, feeling lost, bewildered, distressed, listening to the sound of the two faint voices. Matty must have only been snoozing. He'd been waiting. Waiting for his Uncle Rafael.

He's a good man, she thought. This was no Kass. She could trust him with her son.

Matty's home was in Alp de Ciel. Matty was royal.

But how could she let Matty go again?

And then Rafael was back, returning to warm his hands by the fire. Were they really cold, she wondered, or was it just to give him something to do?

'They'll find Matty here,' she said miserably, going straight to the heart of the matter. 'The press might think Matty's safely at home in Alp de Ciel now, but as soon as they figure he's missing they'll put two and two together. You come out here on a whim. Prince Mathieu disappears at the same time. It'll take them no time at all to figure where Matty might be.'

'And?'

'And I can't protect him here,' she whispered. 'Not from the goldfish bowl that's the royal way of life.'

'So what do you want to do?'

'I don't know.'

'Come back to Alp de Ciel?' he said, and then, at the look on her face, he came to her again. Once again he took her hands in his, his rough, callused hands completely enclosing her smaller ones. 'It's what my mother and I hope for. It's what should happen. That you should come home to the castle.'

'It's not my home.'

'It's your son's home.'

'I hate it.'

'So do I,' he said surprisingly. 'I can't tell you how much I loathe being part of the whole royalty bit. But there's no choice.'

'There must be a choice.'

'If I don't take the Regency on,' he said, 'there are others who would. Others like Kass. You know Kass and his father were lousy rulers. They stripped the country of all they could get their hands on.'

'Of course I know that,' she said angrily. 'But it's nothing to do with me.'

'It is,' he said harshly. 'In as much as it's your son who'll eventually make the decisions about the country's future. If I refuse to take on the Regency, then someone else will take charge until Matty is twenty-five. The next in line is my cousin, Olivier. Olivier is a compulsive gambler. He'd see the Regency as a way to get his hands on the country's coffers. And worse,' he added softly, 'he'd also have absolute say in how Matty is raised. Neither you nor I nor my mother, who until now has been his one constant, would have any influence at all.'

Kelly gasped. 'But…'

'It is unfair,' Rafael said. He was still holding her, using his strength to augment the urgency of what he was saying. 'I know that. But there's not a thing I can do about it. My mother says I don't have a choice and she's right.'

'Your mother…'

'Don't get me wrong. My mother hates the royal bit as much as I do. We're not doing this for personal gain, Kelly.' He hesitated. 'Look, it's too much. I hoped I'd given the press the slip, which would have given you a few days to sort things out. But tomorrow morning the press will be camped outside my accommodation…'

'You're not staying here?'

'How can I?'

'You've gone back to the Prince Edward?'

'I'm being put up in the mayoral residence,' he said ruefully. 'They think I'm home in bed now, getting over jet lag, instead of here, trying to convince you to come with me back to Alp de Ciel.'

'I don't want to.' She sounded like a child—petulant—and she winced but he looked at her with understanding.

'Of course you don't. But this way you'll have your son.'

'There must be another way.'

'There is,' he said reluctantly. 'We could set you up somewhere else, some gated community where you'd be safe. You have all the royal allowance you've never touched, and if it's used to care for Matty even you might swallow your principles and use it. But you'd be even more isolated than you are here.'

'I'm not isolated.'

'I think you are,' he said softly. 'You've been so badly hurt that you've run, not just back to

Australia but back in time. Kelly, you're the mother of the Crown Prince of Alp de Ciel. You knew that when you bore Matty. The crown is his birthright, and it's your duty to be his mother.'

'But your mother loves him. His Aunt Laura…'

'Are you saying you don't want to be his mother?'

'No, I…'

'He doesn't know you yet,' Rafael said. 'He will. He's already proud of what you do—fascinated. He already thinks you're beautiful. Trust takes time, and so does love. Kelly, can you give that to him?'

'But to go back…'

To where she'd been stripped of everything that was important to her—her heart, her pride, her son. How could she go back?

'You won't be alone. My mother will be there.' The grip on her hands grew stronger. 'You didn't meet her last time. She comes across to Manhattan in the worst of Alp de Ciel's winter and spends time with me. You were at the castle for only six weeks after the old prince died, in the last stages of your pregnancy and after Mathieu's birth. The fuss was such that my mother stayed longer with me and when she returned your son was there but you were gone. You'll love her.'

'I don't do love,' she snapped and he stilled.

'Are you saying you don't love Matty?'

'Of…of course…'

'Of course you do,' he agreed softly. 'Love isn't something you can turn on and off again at will.'

'And you know this how?'

He winced. A shadow of pain crossed his face and she thought, I know nothing about him. Nothing. A toy-maker from Manhattan. The Prince Regent of Alp de Ciel.

Rafael.

'You need to come,' he said softly but she was replaying the conversation over in her head, trying to sort it out. There was something not right.

You won't be alone. My mother will be there.

'Will you be there?' she asked. She'd hit a nerve. A muscle moved at the side of his mouth. Infinitesimal—but there was something.

'I'll be there when I need to be.'

'You'll be there when you need to be.' She almost gasped. 'Prince Regent of Alp de Ciel…a country that's desperate for reorganization… There when you need to be?'

'Yes.'

'So…once a week? A week a year?'

'I'm not sure.'

'Then I'm not going,' she said flatly, suddenly sure that she was right. 'The minute I step into the goldfish bowl there'll be no going back. I know how hard it was to shake the press off last time. I had to change my name, change my country, change my whole way of life. I can't do it twice. And you… You'll be there when you can. What sort of commitment is that?'

'Do you want me to be there?'

'No. No!' She should pull away from his hands but she didn't. What she was trying to say was too important. She almost needed personal contact to get it through.

'You're asking me to trust,' she said softly, thinking it as she spoke. 'You're asking me to take my place in a role I hate. Yet you want to be a part-time prince. There's no such thing.'

'Kelly…'

'Your toy workshops could be relocated to Alp de Ciel, couldn't they?'

'Yes, but…'

'And that way the pressure's off Matty,' she said, suddenly more certain of her ground.

'You're Prince Regent. You'll be swanning round the country doing Prince Regent things. Going to movie premières with gorgeous women in tow.'

'Hey!'

'You're not married already, are you?' she demanded and looked down at his ring finger. 'Tell me you're not married.'

'I'm not married.'

'Engaged?'

'No.'

'There you are, then,' she said. 'No celebrity magazine in its right mind will focus on Matty when one of the world's most eligible bachelors is doing his thing in the country.'

'So let me get this straight,' he said faintly. 'You want me to stay permanently in the country and provide fodder for the gossipmongers for the next twenty years to keep the limelight off you and Matty.'

'Yes.'

He blinked. 'I don't…'

But she wasn't to be interrupted. 'If neither of us return,' she said, thinking it through, 'if I don't take Matty back and you return to Manhattan, there'll be no royal permanently in the palace. Which is, I gather, unthinkable. That's why contracts stipulating Matty belonged to the palace were meant to be watertight. Even in my short time with Kass I learned the alternative was chaos. Kass said his father was stuck with him. If he didn't go home the government converted to rule through Council. The Council's been corrupt for generations. Only a prince residing permanently in the country keeps the Principality from turmoil.'

'Which is why we need Matty to stay at the castle.' Rafael tugged his hands back from hers and raked his fingers though his thick black curls. 'Hell, Kelly, I don't want to stay there permanently.'

'Neither do I.'

'It's your…'

'Duty?' Her green eyes flashed anger. 'Don't dare give me that. I wasn't born into royalty like you were. I was lied to, I was married in an attempt to infuriate the old prince and I was kicked out of the country. You said you came here to give me my son. More lies. How dare you say I have a duty now?'

'You have a duty to your son.'

'As you have a duty to the child who will be Crown Prince. Snap.'

'But…'

'There's no but, Rafael,' she said grimly. 'I have no idea what I'm getting into. More than anything in the world, I want to be with Matty, to watch him grow up, to be his mother. I'm willing to sacrifice a lot for that. But not everything. He will not be the total royal focus.'

'You can't ask that of me.'

'I'm not asking. As you're not asking me to be Matty's mother. I'm simply stating facts. You came here to offer me my child back. That's what you said. But you're making no such offer. Not really. You're simply blackmailing me into returning to the castle.'

'I am giving you Matty back.'

'With no strings?'

'He's the Crown Prince of Alp de Ciel. Of course there are strings. Hell, Kelly…I didn't come here to be pressured.'

'No, you came here to pressure me. If you don't like what I'm saying, you can leave. I'll do what I think best with Matty.'

'Which is?'

'It's none of your business.'

'It is my business,' he snapped, exploding. 'Hell, woman, I have total control. According to the contracts you signed, I can take him back tomorrow. I thought I'd give you the choice.'

'No, you didn't. You thought you'd persuade me to come.'

'You're supposed to be *meek*!'

There was a loaded pause. It went on. And on. And on.

'Funny, that,' she said at last, almost cordially. 'I'm not.'

'I can see you're not,' he snapped, goaded.

'You want me to be meek?'

'I want you to be sensible.'

'What's sensible about living as royalty?'

'It's every girl's dream.'

'Hey, I've lived the dream, remember?' she said. 'It's not a dream. It's a nightmare.'

'Which is why I don't want…'

'To be part of it. Neither do I.'

'You have to be.'

'So do you,' she snapped. 'I've been thinking and thinking, all day while I've been waiting for you. I know I can't bring Matty up as I'd want him brought up here. There'll be too much media attention when people realise who he is. I know I can't give him a normal childhood. To haul him away from everything he knows…'

'So you will come?' he demanded, starting to sound relieved.

'Only if you agree to stay permanently in the castle.'

'That's not fair.'

'It is fair,' she snapped. 'It's entirely fair. It's your inheritance—Prince Regent. It's your responsibility to take the pressure off Matty until he's twenty-five. If he stays here, even if we buy into a gated community, he'll be cloistered and not able to have a normal boyhood. And he'll miss you and your mother desperately. But if he goes back to the castle and you head off back to your very important life in the States it'll be much, much worse. So *fair* doesn't come into it. We're both having to do what we do to survive. I won't have Matty in the limelight any more than he has to be.'

'You mean *you* don't want to be in the limelight.'

'Of course I don't. Neither do you, but from where I'm standing you're the one who can take it best.'

'You know nothing about what I can take.'

'Ditto,' she snapped. 'I'm making judgements. But, the way I see it, there are two of us I'm protecting. Me and Matty. You think I'll let you stand aside and leave Matty exposed?'

'No, I…'

'You came here saying I was welcome to keep Matty with me,' she said. 'If I did that you'd be stuck.'

'I never imagined…'

'That I wouldn't jump at the chance to be princess again? I can see that.'

'Kelly…' He reached for her hands again and held them urgently.

'Rafael.'

This was ludicrous. It was like some weird tug of war. But she wasn't giving in. The thought of staying in the castle as the Princess Royal, of having all that media directed at her and her small son… She'd been through that. She never wanted to go there again.

She didn't care about this man's story. She couldn't care that there might be valid reasons for him to wish to avoid the limelight. She had to make a decision now and she could only do that on the information she had.

He was gripping her hands with a strength that almost frightened her. How had that happened? With the linking of their hands he seemed almost an extension of herself—she was arguing with herself instead of him.

But…it was different. The feel of his hands on hers was doing strange things to her. It was feeding her strength, she thought obliquely. If he withdrew his hands she might falter. She might not have the strength to stand up to him.

She held on and his grip tightened still more, as if it were the same for him.

'Kelly, you can do it,' he said urgently and she shook her head.

'Rafael, you can do it.'

'I don't…'

'Neither do I. And my reasons are better than yours,' she said. 'As far as I know. Is there anything you're not telling me?'

'No!'

'There you are, then.'

'It's blackmail,' he snapped and she shook her head.

'It's no such thing. It's sense. You bring your toys and you come home.'

Home. The word drifted between them, strangely poignant.

Rafael stared down into her eyes, seemingly baffled. She met his gaze firmly, unflinching. Did he know he was feeding her strength with his hold? she thought. Why didn't he pull away?

She didn't want him to pull away. She had a feeling that if she did… Well, the world was a huge and scary place. To think about going back…to relive the terror…

She couldn't do it alone. She had to have an ally.

And this man could be an ally. She'd grown up enormously over the last five years. Men like Kass… Well, he'd taught her a hard life lesson but she'd learned it well. Never again would she throw her heart in the ring but, as well as that, she'd also learned to judge. In these last few years she'd learned who her true friends were. And this man…

This man was trustworthy. There were things in his background she didn't understand. There were shadows—real shadows—and they must be linked to his revulsion at taking on the Prince Regent role, but the sensation that he was solid, that he was a man of his word, was growing rather than receding.

His disinclination to take on the Prince Regency did him no disservice in her eyes. How could anyone want such a job?

How could she return to that lifestyle?

'It's an awful thing you're asking me to do,' she whispered. 'To go back and be part of royalty again. But you've brought the only enticement that could ever get me there—my son. I have to be deeply, profoundly grateful, and I am. But not enough to do this on my own, Rafael. I need you there.'

'You don't need me.'

'Well, maybe you're right. Maybe I don't need anyone,' she conceded. 'I've made sure of that over these last five years. But this is different. It's not you personally. I need your presence. I need there to be a sovereign to take the limelight from Matty. Maybe you made a mistake bringing him here, offering what you've offered. But you have offered it. And…and I made a call this afternoon. I phoned immigration.'

'*You what?*'

'I can keep him right here, whether you say so or not, and under my terms,' she said, jutting her chin forward in a dumb gesture of defiance. 'A contract signed in Alp de Ciel holds no weight here when it comes to child custody rights. I'm Matty's mother and he has no father. Matty is in Australia. You brought him to me—his Australian mother—for which I'm profoundly thankful but now…you can't change your mind and take him back. The laws of this country will support me.'

He stared down at her, baffled. Whatever route he'd planned this conversation to take, it clearly wasn't this one.

'I only wanted you to have your son back,' he said and he sounded so bewildered that she smiled.

'You did. It was lovely of you.'

'I assumed you'd want to come back.'

'That was sweet of you too, but silly.'

'I don't believe,' he said cautiously, 'that silly comes into it. Or sweet either, for that matter.'

'Regardless…sweet or silly…you will stay permanently in Alp de Ciel?'

'Hell, Kelly…'

'I know,' she said. 'That's royalty. I hate it and I want no part in it but maybe I'm prepared to take it on for Matty's sake. He does stand to inherit one day and I realize it'd be very much better if he was brought up in the environment he'll have to face. But for you… Like Matty, you don't have a choice. You're Prince Regent, like it or not. We do this together, Rafael, or not at all.'

'I can't.'

'Then neither can I,' she said implacably, and waited.

He stared down into her eyes. She met his gaze, unflinching. He didn't really look like his cousin, she thought. The resemblance was only superficial. Kass's eyes had been piercing, brutal, cold. Rafael's…They were troubled now. Shadowed.

She knew she was forcing him to go where he had no wish to tread, but she had no choice. All afternoon the alternatives had been slamming at her, one after another.

There wasn't an alternative. She knew it.

Rafael knew it.

'You will take some of the limelight,' he said, sounding desperate, and she smiled.

'They can photograph me if they want, but I'll bet you have women on your arm more glamorous than I'll ever be.'

'I don't do glamour.'

'Says the man who just walked into my cottage wearing a dress sword.'

'Kelly…'

'Rafael.'

'You really are serious.'

'I really am serious.'

'So I get to stay in Alp de Ciel until Matty turns twenty-five?'

'There you go, then,' she said, trying to sound cheerful. 'It's only a twenty-year sentence. Whereas I…'

'You can leave any time.'

'Sure,' she said. 'You let Matty sleep in my bed and then you tell me I can leave any time. My sentence is as long as yours, Rafael, maybe even longer.'

There was a loaded pause. They were still holding hands. It was as if the urgency of their conversation required physical contact as well as verbal.

'Fine,' he said at last. 'Okay, then. But it is blackmail.'

'On both our sides,' she said gently. 'We're forced into this.'

'The palace doesn't need us both.'

'No,' she said wearily. 'But as it's both or neither then we might as well get on with it. And Matty…Matty needs someone. I'm hoping it might be me, but for now he needs you. I'll fight for that too, Rafael. I'll fight for what my son needs.'

It caught him. Something in her voice made him pause. He tugged sharply at her hands, forcing her to look up at him.

'Kelly, it's not really a life sentence,' he said.

'You know it is.'

'It might even be fun.'

'Says the man who wants to flee to Manhattan.'

'We could make it fun.'

'Like how?'

His mouth twisted. 'Don't ask me.' He glanced at his wrist-watch and grimaced. 'I need to go. Any minute now the dinner will end and there'll be questions as to why I'm not in the royal bed.'

'Matty will miss you when he wakes.'

'Remind him you're his mother,' he said softly. Then, at the look on her face, he said more urgently, 'It's the truth. You are his mother. You love him already and his love will come.'

'I don't think…'

'No, don't think,' he said urgently. 'That's the way of madness. One day at a time. Starting now. We can do this.' And then, before she knew what he was about, he'd caught her chin with his fingers and forced her face up to meet his. His mouth lowered on hers in a swift, demanding kiss.

It shocked them both. She could feel it, like a stab of white-hot heat coming from nowhere. It lasted seconds, hardly even that, and then it was over but, as he released her, her hands flew to her lips and she gazed up at him in bewilderment.

Where had that come from? Why on earth…?

He was looking as bewildered as she was. As if some force other than his had propelled the kiss. As if he, too, didn't understand what had just happened.

'I guess it's a pact,' he said at last as he stepped back and she gazed at him in stupefaction. 'A kiss to seal a bargain.'

'A handshake would have done,' she whispered.

'Nah,' he said and suddenly he grinned and it was like the sun had come out. He was suddenly like a kid in mischief. 'Where's the fun in a handshake? A kiss is much more satisfactory. Don't look like that, Your Highness. I meant no disrespect.'

'I didn't think…'

'It's just as well you don't think,' he said. 'As the mother of the Crown Prince, you could probably have my head skewered and served on a platter for breakfast for doing what I just did. So let's just forget the kiss. Good though it was.' He lifted his dress sword and slid it into its scabbard. His smile faded.

'So, like it or not, we have a deal. We're in this together, Kellyn Marie. I won't see you now until we leave. Can you be ready to return with me on Tuesday? Yes? Unless you want to be overrun with media before then, I shouldn't return here, and now I'm outed I'll have to do the full diplomatic round. Tell Matty I love him, and tell him he has a mother in a million.'

'Even if she's a blackmailing cow.'

'She's not so bad for a blackmailing cow,' he said and grinned. 'I've seen worse things come out of cheese.'

What the hell had he done?

Rafael walked out through the darkened historical village and thought he must have gone completely mad.

He'd just agreed to stay in Alp de Ciel until Matty was twenty-five.

He didn't have to. He could promise and then leave anyway once Matty was safely back in the country.

He couldn't. He thought back to Kelly's face by the firelight. She trusted him.

He was trustworthy. Hell!

He'd kissed her.

Why had he done that?

It was just that she was so damned kissable. She was such a juxtaposition of sweet, meek and...dragon, he thought ruefully. Life had slapped her around and that was what she looked like, that was how she sounded, but underneath there was a fierce and determined sprite.

What had Kass been thinking to treat her so appallingly?

She'd just blackmailed him into moving his life to Alp de Ciel.

His mother would be delighted.

But Anna…

Whoops.

He needed to talk to Anna before she learned of things via the media, he thought. Kelly might come across as a bit of a dragon but that was nothing to how Anna came across when she was angry.

Would Anna relocate to Alp de Ciel?

Ha.

Too hard. It was all just too hard.

Pete was on the gate, obviously waiting for him to leave. Rafael tugged a note from his wallet to leave him something for his pains, but Pete shook his head at the offering as if he was personally offended.

'I don't want your money.'

'I'm sorry,' Rafael said, surprised.

'I just don't want you mucking our Kelly about,' Pete said strongly. 'She's had a rough trot, our Kell.'

'You could help by not telling anyone I was here tonight. And not telling anyone Kelly has a strange little boy staying with her.'

'You think I'd do that?'

'No,' Rafael said with a faint smile.

'You really are a prince?' the old man demanded, and Rafael nodded.

'Yes.'

'And the wee one…'

'He's Kelly's son,' Rafael said, for there was no use dissembling here. 'The Crown Prince of Alp de Ciel.'

Pete gave a long, low whistle. 'Well, I'll be damned. Our Kelly, royalty. We always knew there was something…' But then he returned to what had obviously been gnawing at him. 'She's upset. Anyone can see she's upset.'

'It's been a harrowing day for her.'

'You'll be taking her back to…where…Alp de Wotsit?'

'She's agreed to go, yes.'

'Then I'll say something to you now, boy,' the old man growled and, dress sword or not, Rafael found himself backed against the wall with the old man's gnarled finger poking him in the midriff. 'You take care of her. She's gone through the mill, that one. Oh, we're not supposed to know, but there's not many of the staff here don't know that she lost her kiddy. We thought maybe he'd died. She's wanted to be anonymous, she hasn't wanted to talk about it, and we've respected that. We'd keep her secret for as long as she wants. But this place is almost family. She might not have a mum and dad but she has all of us and if she's mistreated we'll… we'll…'

'Send the dragoons?' Rafael asked faintly, and the old man relented a little and gave a crooked smile.

'Yeah, well, the troops we have here may only be make-believe but we can surely make a fuss. So watch it. Watch her.'

'She'll be okay.'

'You guarantee it, sir?'

Now there was an ask. What was he letting himself into? As Prince Regent he was responsible for the well-being of the Crown Prince. Now he was being asked to make guarantees about Kelly.

But Pete was waiting, and behind the belligerence was anxiety. He was genuinely fond of her, Rafael thought. He was genuinely anxious.

So once again he promised. 'I guarantee she'll be okay.'

'You'll watch over her.'

And stay permanently in Alp de Ciel? With or without Anna? With or without his business?

Anna would kill him. To make such a decision without talking it through with her... But the decision was made.

'I'll watch over her,' he said weakly, and thought, Anna without Fifth Avenue? Without pastrami on rye? His business without Anna?

'I'll watch over her,' he promised again and he was allowed to leave.

But the pressure of Pete's finger in his chest stayed with him. Pressure... Hell!

He'd kissed her.

How had that happened? Why? Kelly watched Rafael disappear down the main street towards the exit, then started to get ready for bed. She undressed by the fire, thinking that she didn't want to get undressed in her bedroom yet. Matty was too much a stranger. Her little boy...

It was set. She was going back to Alp de Ciel to take her place as mother of the Crown Prince.

Rafael had kissed her.

She raised a finger to her lips. They still felt bruised, which was crazy. He hadn't kissed her hard enough to bruise.

But she could still feel where he'd kissed her.

She tugged her nightgown on, then sank into the rocker by the stove, flipped open the fire door and watched the flames. To leave here…

The thought was terrifying.

She had to leave on Tuesday.

There was no choice. She'd known that the moment she'd set eyes on Matty. No matter what she had to do, now she'd seen her son again she would move heaven and earth rather than endure further separation.

Rafael had kissed her.

'And that was stupid,' she told herself fiercely. 'That's enough of that. You've let no man touch you since Kass and you'd be crazy to break that rule now. And with a de Boutaine? No and no and no.'

On impulse she crossed to her desk and booted her computer. Her nineteenth-century cottage boasted wireless Internet—hooray. She typed in Rafael's name and waited.

There was too much to take in. It was mostly about his work, his toys, awards he'd won, speeches he'd given. He ran some youth apprentice training scheme—very worthy.

She was becoming cynical in her old age, she thought ruefully, and then decided she'd had enough of reading about him.

She clicked on Google Images.

The first one that appeared was at a gala charity event in New York. There was Rafael, looking impossibly handsome in a magnificently cut, deep black dinner suit and a classy white silk scarf.

And on his arm was a stunner—a woman whose legs almost seemed to reach her armpits. She was a magnificent, classy blonde and she was clinging to Rafael's arm and smiling possessively at him as he smiled at the camera.

The caption read 'Rafael de Boutaine and his partner, Anna Louise St Clair.'

'Well, there you go, then,' she muttered to herself. 'He has a partner.'

He'd said he wasn't married or engaged.

He had a partner.

For someone completely disinterested, there was no way of explaining the sudden lurch of loss she felt in the pit of her stomach.

'It's only that he'd suit my purpose better if

he's a real bachelor,' she told herself. 'He'd get more media attention.'

And then she looked again at Anna and thought, Nope, gaining media attention was never going to be a problem for these two. The pair would be the ruling couple of Alp de Ciel.

'Which is what you want,' she said fiercely, slamming down the lid of her computer. 'How dumb are you to ask if he's married or engaged?' she demanded of herself as she headed for bed. 'How quaint. It's just as well I'm a historian because that's what I feel like.' She stopped herself from tossing a pillow at the wall just in time. For Matty was sleeping. Her Matty. Who this was all about.

'So it'll suit our purpose,' she told her sleeping son, lowering her voice to a whisper. 'It's just that he kissed me, Matty. How crazy's that? And I let him. I must be going out of my mind.'

CHAPTER FOUR

Was there ever any doubt she'd go with him? Whether Rafael had a partner or not was immaterial. Matty belonged in Alp de Ciel. Matty was her son.

She was going.

So over the next few days Kelly packed her gear, said goodbye to the place that had protected her for the last five years and prepared to be a princess again.

She still was the Princess Kellyn, she thought ruefully. Kass had never bothered with divorce. In truth, it had suited Kass to remain married. He had the heir he needed so what purpose marriage? He'd been able to play around with as many women as he'd wanted.

While Kelly hadn't worn a wedding ring for five years, Kass had worn his to the end. He'd married her as a snub to his father. His continuing marriage had been a snub to any eligible woman in the Principality who might have been presumptuous enough to think of joining him on the throne.

So, regardless of Kass's motives, Kelly was now returning as the widow of the old Crown Prince and the mother of the new one. Somehow she had to make a life for herself in a country she loathed. She had no idea how she was going to do it, but she had no choice.

At least her departure was managed without media hype. Whatever the staff of the park knew of her past or of her intentions now, they were saying nothing to the outside world, giving her a few blessed days to come to terms with what she must do.

Rafael couldn't come near them. He rang when he could but the media attention meant that he had to stay well away. So Kelly had a few short days to think about what life might have been if Matty wasn't a prince.

It would have been magic.

For Matty was absorbed into the life of the park as seamlessly as if he'd been born there. For the first twenty-four hours he was homesick for Rafael, but the park kids—the children of the staff here—were friendly and eager to show him

everything. There were things going on everywhere and by the time they were ready to leave
he was simply part of the park pack.

She so wished he could stay like this. He was
mischievous, inquisitive, alert and interested.
Once he was reassured that Rafael hadn't
deserted him, that there was a definite end to his
stay, he was totally relaxed, and Kelly thought,
If only he could stay, if only…

But it was impossible. No one had yet twigged
that the Crown Prince was missing from Alp de
Ciel. As soon as they did, it'd be only a matter
of days before he was found and he'd never be
let alone again.

So they had to go. She felt sick at the thought
and even Matty was crestfallen on Tuesday as
they prepared to leave.

'Uncle Rafael will cheer us up,' Matty said,
holding her hand as they walked together for the
last time from her cottage down to the park
entrance. 'Don't be sad, Mama. He'll make you
happy again.'

Terrific. Although Kelly was fighting really
hard to blink back tears, she had no desire to have
Rafael to buoy her spirits. In truth, the fact that
she'd be travelling with Rafael was a

downside—he made her feel disconcerted and vulnerable.

And she'd miss this place so much… She was so close to breaking it was all she could do to walk those last few steps from the park gates to the waiting limousine. To where Rafael was waiting, holding the door wide for her.

He was watching her with sympathy, she thought as she dashed her hand across her eyes with a fierce anger that was surely irrational. The last thing she needed was sympathy, but it shouldn't make her angry.

'Hey,' he said as Matty reached him. He stooped down and hugged Matty hard and that had Kelly blinking all over again. Then he straightened and looked at Kelly. He was dressed formally—not in his dumb dress uniform but in a smart grey lounge suit. 'Are you okay?' he asked softly.

'I'm fine.' She gulped a couple of times and turned to help Pete, who was putting her luggage into the trunk. 'Where's… where's your retinue?'

'Retinue?'

'Reporters. Cameramen.'

'Thankfully my presence doesn't warrant the type of paparazzi outriders Princess Di was burdened with,' he said, smiling. 'I'd imagine there'll be photographers at the airport but that's okay—we'll be in the door, on the plane and out of here before they realize we have Matty.' He hesitated as she hugged Pete goodbye. 'Kelly, you're sure you're okay?'

'I'm okay,' she said, feeling sick. She dived past him into the car and slid across the vast leather interior of the limousine until she was as far away from his side as it was possible to be. Matty was on the opposite seat, but as Rafael climbed in after her he sidled across to Rafael and sat hard against him.

Rafael tugged him close, which had Kelly unsettled all over again. Her son was being hugged by Rafael. Whatever decisions she'd made about the man, she still couldn't entirely trust him. He was too damned good-looking. He was a prince. He was a de Boutaine!

She crossed her arms and didn't say anything. He was hugging her son. Her son! How could she catch up on five long years?

'So you've decided to go casual,' he said politely as the chauffeur drove the big car out on to the road.

'What…what do you mean?'

'It's the first time I've seen you in civvies.'

'You mean not in historical dress.'

'Mmm.'

'Is something wrong with what I'm wearing?'

'You'll be landing in Alp de Ciel like that?' he asked gently. 'Or do you intend to keep something separate from your luggage to change into?'

'Why should I?'

'I would have thought…'

'Thought what?'

'Maybe a little more formality?'

'I'm fine like I am,' she said, keeping her arms folded defensively across her breasts and glaring straight ahead.

In truth she was making a statement. She'd stared at her wardrobe last night for almost an hour before she'd decided what to wear.

For the last four years Kelly had worn almost exclusively historical costumes. However, there had been times when she'd been out doing research, when she had given presentations about the park, when she had attended awards dinners, when she'd had to wear normal clothes. Then she'd worn a standard business suit. Sensible.

Once upon a time she'd loved clothes. She'd ached for them. When she was a child her parents had frowned on what they called frivolity. She'd been repressed to the point of cruelty, forced to wear her school uniform when it had been entirely inappropriate, given a meagre allowance that had been inadequate to buy anything but the basic necessities.

She remembered the dress she'd bought with her first pay cheque. It was a sliver of scarlet, an almost indecently short crimson cocktail dress. She'd loved it.

She'd worn it to dinner the first night she'd met Kass.

Yeah, well, so much for fancy clothes. Like horses, clothes were something she didn't let herself think about. Now she was wearing ancient jeans, an oversized, shapeless sweater that reached almost to her knees and her leather work boots. She'd tugged her hair into a knot with an elastic band. She was wearing no make-up.

Yes, it was a statement and she didn't care who heard it.

'Mama packed most of her clothes into boxes and sent them to storage,' Matty offered from the other seat.

Rafael frowned. 'I told you to pack them up for shipping.'

'It's no use shipping historical costumes overseas,' Kelly said. 'I'm bringing what I need.'

'So did you send anything to the shipping company I told you about?'

'No.'

'So let me see,' Rafael said faintly. 'You're moving to Alp de Ciel permanently. And you've got…one suitcase?'

'It's summer there right now. If it's cold later on I may have to buy a couple of things. I assume there are still shops.'

'There are shops,' he said, eyeing her sweater with a certain amount of trepidation. 'But there'll be media meeting us off the plane. Do you have…a frock or something?'

'A frock,' she said, and her lips twitched at his obvious discomfort. 'I don't believe I do have a frock.'

'You know what I mean. Something respectable.'

'This is respectable.'

'For bumming round the stables maybe. Not for meeting your people.'

'Whose people?'

'You're a princess.'

'In name only,' she retorted. 'I thought we agreed. You're the centre of media attention. You wear your braid and your dress sword and I'll wear my sweater and jeans.'

'It's not very pretty,' Matty said, disapproving.

'I don't need to be pretty.'

'No, but you are,' Matty said, sounding upset. 'And you're my mama.'

Oh, great. She hadn't thought this one through. It was all very well planning to be plain Jane, speaking when spoken to, staying in the background, keeping herself small.

But Matty was obviously disappointed.

'You can't do that to the kid,' Rafael said and she swallowed her vague guilt and thought, what was she asking? That Matty cope with a mama who didn't dress like…like Rafael's partner.

'You're saying my wearing jeans might damage Matty for life?'

'No, I…'

'Good then. I'm fine,' she muttered. 'This is me. This is who I am. Matty, I'm sorry if you don't like it but I don't want to be a princess. I'm your mama and I hope you like me anyway but I'm not going to wear a tiara. Not for anything.'

'How about a frock?' Rafael growled and she glowered.

'Nope. Matty, you and your Uncle Rafael are

royalty,' she said bluntly. 'I get to stay in the background and watch.'

'You'll watch?' Rafael demanded, incredulous.

'Yes.'

'You don't think you might get bored?' Rafael said.

'No.'

'What will you do, then?' Matty asked while Rafael looked on with bemusement. He seemed to be having trouble figuring her out, which was fine as she was having trouble figuring him out. All she knew about him was that, in his own way, he was as dangerous to her peace of mind as Kass had been. He was a de Boutaine and he'd kissed her. That was enough for her to stay in sackcloth and ashes every time she was near him for the next hundred years. To do anything else…that was the crazy route.

'I've thought about it,' she said seriously, having in fact done little over the last three days but think about how she could sustain the life they were asking her to lead. 'I'm intending to write books.'

'Books,' Rafael said blankly.

'That's the plan,' she said happily. 'Matty, I'm a historian and your castle is steeped in history. I can find myself a nice quiet attic and research to my heart's content. But I'll be there for you whenever you need me, Matty—if you need me. Otherwise, I'll be perfectly happy writing my book.'

'You can't,' Rafael said blankly.

'Why not?'

'I was hoping…'

'Don't hope,' she said bluntly. 'Alp de Ciel is your principality, not mine. Stop hoping for anything from me, other than loving Matty. For that's all I'm going to do.'

They let her be.

They travelled first class on the aircraft—of course—which meant the seats were in pairs, cocoons that turned into beds. Rafael and Matty shared one pair. A Japanese businessman shared Kelly's. She was courteously given the window seat, which meant that she was buffered from the pair across the aisle.

She hardly talked to them.

Rafael and Matty slept. She stared straight ahead, feeling sick.

Finally they landed. There were photographers, reporters, politicians, all waiting. They were stunned to see Matty.

Kelly hung back, trying to blend in as part of the luggage. She was afraid that Rafael would haul her forward and introduce her but he did no such thing. At the last minute, as the limousine was about to leave, he motioned for her to join them and she slid into the car before the photographers could register who she might be.

Now she was doing the defensive bit again, huddled in the far corner of the car, staring out at the countryside.

Remembering how she'd fallen in love with this country the first time she'd seen it.

She'd forgotten how breathtaking it was.

She'd forgotten how she'd fallen in love.

The four Alp countries had been severed from their larger neighbours centuries ago to form principalities for warring brothers, and each one of them was a magical place in its own right.

Alp de Ciel…Alps towering to the skies.

Even though it was late spring there was still snow on the highest peaks. The lowlands stretching from the coast to the mountains consisted of magnificent undulating pastures, rich and fertile. There were quaint villages, houses hewn from the local rock hugging the coastline, some of the houses seemingly carved from the cliffs themselves. There were harbours with fishing fleets that looked straight off picture postcards. Too small to involve itself in the world wars, too insignificant to be fought over, Alp de Ciel had remained almost unchanged for centuries.

The first time Kelly had seen it she'd been speechless with delight and it affected her just as deeply now. She stared out of the car window as they left the port city, then followed the river road to the foothills of the mountains, through Zunderfied, the small village which had served the castle for generations and then further to where the palace of Alp de Ciel lay in all its glory.

It was no wonder she'd fallen for Kass, an older and wiser Kelly thought sadly. This place breathed romance. She'd been lonely and awed and in love with this country—Kass must have found her more than ripe for the picking.

She couldn't let herself be swayed by beauty this time. Nor by words.

Nor by a de Boutaine…

'It's not all as beautiful as it looks,' Rafael told her as she sat with her nose squashed against the window, and she cast him a look that was almost scared.

'It *is* beautiful.'

'Surface gorgeous. You know how Kass financed his latest bout of gambling debts? He allowed logging almost to the edge of Zunderfied. The land here gets saturated with the snow melts. We've had two minor landslips there with spring already. That's just one problem among hundreds.'

She turned and gazed upward and saw the scarred hillside, the jarring ugliness of the leavings from clear felling. But…to allow herself to worry about the countryside…the people…

She wasn't royal. She wasn't!

She mustn't care.

'You love it,' Rafael said softly as the car slowed and turned into the palace grounds.

'Not…not any more.'

'There's no need to be defensive,' he said. 'There's no one who wants you to do anything you don't want. I dare say the villagers can worry about their landslips very well themselves without you worrying on their behalf.' He grimaced. 'If you want to cloister yourself in your attic in your remarkable sweater then your wish will be respected.'

'Does that mean Mama is allowed to wear that sweater?' Matty demanded, astounded.

'It's her business.'

'Ellen will say it's not royal.'

'Ellen will say no such thing,' Rafael said firmly. 'Your mother is here as her own person. She can do exactly as she pleases.'

Damn, why was she blinking again? She glanced out of the back window of the car and saw the tiny township of Zunderfied perched below a swathe of freshly cleared mountainside. She'd boarded there when she'd first come here and thought it was delightful—a tiny alpine village that was steeped in history.

But the logging... How could Kass have agreed to such a thing? Even from here it seemed the little town was in peril. She wanted to get out of the car and start replanting *now*.

No! NMP, she told herself fiercely.

Not My Problem.

There was no hiding in the background when they arrived at the palace. She was expected.

The first time she'd arrived here it had been with the archaeological dig team. They'd worked out of sight of the main castle, sifting through the remains of ancient castle sites. So the only time she'd been in this forecourt had been the time she'd arrived with Kass.

She'd been eight months pregnant. Her pregnancy had been dreadful. She'd been sick all the time, and Kass had hardly been near.

But then his father was dead and he was triumphant. He'd hauled her home, almost as a trophy.

'This is my wife,' he'd said, tugging her out of the limousine and not caring that she almost fell. 'She's carrying my heir. A son. This is now my country. *My country.*'

The domestic staff had all been there to greet him—they'd lined up on either side of the castle entrance. She remembered the silence. The silent, cold disapproval.

Kass had swept inside, leaving her to follow.

'Take care of her,' he'd snapped to a couple of the domestic staff. 'She's to have everything she needs to deliver a perfect child.'

It had stayed with her. The dismay in the eyes of everyone around her. The contempt. Even…pity?

But now…

This was very, very different.

Yes, the staff were assembled. Not as many. It was a pared down staff, maybe only a quarter as big.

Every one of the staff was smiling.

'Ellen,' Matty yelled, launching himself out of the car and heading straight for a buxom woman at the end of the line. Then, as she scooped him into her arms and hugged, he turned from her shoulder and whooped as he saw more friends, 'Marguerite. Aunt Laura.'

They were all beaming at her little son. Rafael was smiling too. A man she remembered… Crater—the palace Secretary of State, more stooped than she remembered and his hair more silver—was stepping forward to grasp Rafael's hand.

'It's good to have you back, sir.'

'It's good to be back,' Rafael said. He turned to hug a woman near him—a lady around the same age as Crater. She was wearing a flowing skirt, a cardigan that reached almost to her knees and a paint-spattered pinafore over everything. Her abundance of silver hair was tied up in a knot and there was paint there too. She was smiling with everyone else but sniffing into a paint-smudged handkerchief.

'Mama, don't you dare cry.' He picked her up and whirled her round as he might have whirled a child. 'I've been away only a week. Kelly will think you're soppy.'

'Kelly,' the lady whispered and Rafael set her down and turned her to face Kelly.

'Mama, this is Kelly. Everyone, this is our own Princess Kellyn Marie de Boutaine. She's been sorely wronged but she's finally consented to take her place where she ought to be. It gives me huge pleasure to tell you all that our Kelly has finally come home.'

And for a moment—for just a moment—Kelly wished she looked more like a princess. The last thing she wanted was to be thought of as a poor relation. She hadn't thought it through...

But she couldn't think it for long for Laura gave her no chance. With a cry of delight, Laura abandoned Rafael and took swift steps to where she was standing. Kelly could hardly be self-conscious of her clothes in the face of layers of paint. There was even a daub of purple on Laura's left eyebrow.

And there was no disguising the sincerity of her welcome. Smiling warmly, Laura took her by both hands and held her at arm's length, surveying her from head to toe. But Kelly thought she wasn't seeing the clothes. She was looking deeper.

'So you've come home,' Laura whispered. 'Oh, my dear, we are so sorry. This country's done you such a wrong. I don't know how you can ever forgive us, but from now on…we're overjoyed to have you here. Welcome home, Kelly, dear.'

She turned and held Kelly's hand high in hers.

'Our Matty has his mother home,' she said to the assemblage. 'And we have our princess. Thank you, Rafael, for bringing our Kellyn home.'

But of course she wasn't 'our Kellyn'. She'd never been part of this royal family and she had no intention of being slotted neatly into an allocated space now.

The next few hours passed in a haze of shock and confusion and jet lag. Somehow, however, she managed to keep her wits about her enough to insist on her independence from the first.

With the first greetings over, with Matty scampering off to greet his friends, to make sure nothing had changed in his absence and to distribute the myriad of souvenir gifts he'd stocked up on, Laura and Rafael showed her to her rooms. To her horror, she found she was expected to sleep in the same ghastly, opulent suite she'd been confined to while she'd waited for Matty to be born. It had been closed when she left and hadn't been used since. She glanced through to the bathroom and the dressing gown she'd worn when she was pregnant was folded neatly on a side table. Cleaned and pressed. Waiting for her to return?

She backed out in horror. No and no and no.

Rafael raised his eyebrows in bemusement. 'These are the best we have,' he said. 'Rooms fit for a royal bride. Kass never felt any desire to put anyone else in them.'

'Then get yourself a royal bride to put in them,' she said crisply, staring round at the gilt and chandeliers and rich crimson velvet with loathing. 'I think I get to be described as the royal relic from now on. I don't want anything to do with this stuff.'

'You don't look like a relic.'

'If she doesn't want gilt she doesn't have gilt,' Laura said stoutly. 'There's not a scrap of gilt in the dower house. Not that I'm offering to share. It's a wee bit cosy.'

'My mother paints,' Rafael said unnecessarily, smiling at his mother in affection. 'The dower house has five bedrooms. Or it did have five bedrooms. Now it has five studios, one of which has my mother's bed crammed in the corner.' He hesitated, looking at Kelly's face and registering her real distress. 'Meanwhile this lady wants an attic,' Rafael said softly. 'Mama, which are our most respectable attics?'

The staff seemed flummoxed but she was then given a guided tour of the place.

Matty had almost a wing to himself—the palace nurseries. Right above was an attic wing—two rooms with turret windows, facing south, with sunlight streaming in through the ancient, hand-blown glass.

The furnishings were faded. 'I think someone's maiden aunt might have used these rooms a long time ago,' Laura said, looking about her at the doilies and antimacassars and overstuffed arm-chairs. And the tiny narrow bed.

'It's fine,' Kelly said.

'Only if we can get you a new bed,' Rafael growled, so she graciously accepted, asked for a desk and a decent reading light and prepared to start being a recluse.

It didn't quite work straight off. For a start she needed to read Matty his bedtime story. 'For surely that's your role now,' Laura said gently.

It was, and she loved that Laura and Rafael—and Marguerite and Ellen and every one of the palace staff—seemed determined to let her be Matty's mother in every sense of the word.

So she read to Matty in a big armchair in front of the nursery fire. Halfway through the story he sidled on to her knee and promptly fell asleep in her arms. The sensation was indescribable. It almost made her forget her vow to be a recluse.

So she'd be a recluse who did the odd cuddle on the side.

Then supper was ready. 'We waited for you,' Ellen told her and Kelly thought tomorrow she'd figure how she could use the kitchen and make herself toasted sandwiches because that was all she felt like, but tonight she was stuck.

She remembered the grand dining room where she'd been served in the past with pomp and rigid silence. She followed Ellen downstairs with a sinking heart but, instead of being ushered into the grand salon she remembered, Ellen led the way through less formal corridors, down worn stone steps and into…a kitchen. A vast kitchen with a range that took half a wall, with a table big enough to feed a football team, ancient wood, worn with scrubbing.

Laura was sitting at the table buttering bread. Rafael was at the range cooking…toasted sandwiches?

'I wanted to make you dinner myself tonight,'

Laura said, smiling at her obvious discompo-
sure. 'I have a much less grand kitchen. But we
thought Matty would be asleep here and you
might want to stick close.'

'Close?' she queried faintly, thinking of the
corridors she'd just navigated, and Rafael flipped
the sandwich he was toasting and grinned.

'Close in castle terms. Less than half a day's
march. Can we interest you in a toasted cheese
sandwich?'

'What happened to silver service?' she said
faintly and Laura winced.

'Don't say you liked it.'

'No, I…'

'The minute Kass died we locked up the dining
room. Matty hates it, you see,' she explained. 'It
was the only time Matty ever saw his father.
When Kass was in the palace, at the end of every
meal he'd send for Matty and grill him on his
lessons. Matty used to shake every time he
passed the dining room. So we thought we
wouldn't use it.'

'My mother's pretty definite,' Rafael said.
'But, of course, it's your call now. If you want
to use the dining room…'

'It's not my call. It's you who's Prince Regent.'

'If it's up to me, I like it just fine where I am,' he said. 'Actually, no. I like it better in Manhattan but, since I've been blackmailed…'

'You've been no such thing,' Laura retorted. 'Kelly, I refuse to let you feel guilty. Rafael's known from the moment Kass died that his responsibility was here.'

'You want him to stay?'

'No,' Laura said bluntly. 'Well, no, in terms of no, I don't want him to have to assume the mantle of royalty. But in terms of having someone round who can cook great toasted sandwiches…' She smiled, a smile that matched her son's to a T as he flipped a sandwich on to her plate. 'I taught him his culinary skills,' she said proudly. 'It's my greatest feat. He'll make some woman very happy some day. He'll keep her in toasted sandwiches for ever.'

'Does Anna like toasted sandwiches?' Kelly asked before she could stop herself and the two identical grins faded.

'Probably not,' Laura said cautiously.

'You mean definitely not,' Rafael retorted.

'Have you broken the news to Anna that you're relocating here permanently?' his mother asked.

'Nope.'

'Coward.'

'I am a coward,' he admitted and he turned his attention back to his pan. 'You know Anna. You'd be a coward too. Kelly, two sandwiches or more?'

It was a lovely, laughing informal meal, about as different from what she remembered of castle life as it was possible to be. She ate three rounds of toasted cheese sandwiches and a vast bowl of sun-ripened strawberries picked only hours ago from the palace gardens. Then Rafael made coffee using a mysterious Turkish coffee-maker that he swore made coffee that was a legend in its own time.

It was pretty good coffee. It was pretty good company. Kelly said little, content to listen to Laura and her son catch up on castle gossip, on trivial domestic stuff, on a life she was starting to feel maybe wouldn't be as bad as she'd thought it would be.

'I need to go,' Laura said reluctantly after the coffee was finished and the plates were cleared into the sink. 'Rafael has a deputation to meet at eight and I don't want to be around when they come.'

'A deputation?'

'Just a welcome home committee,' Rafael said and grimaced. 'The mayor and the town's dignitaries welcoming me home. Or, more probably, to make sure I know the deforestation issue is urgent. Plus about a thousand other grievances. They wanted to come in the morning but my gear's coming so they've agreed to come tonight.' He hesitated. 'They won't meet with Crater. They see him as part of the old establishment. Which leaves me. I wouldn't mind some support.'

'You're a big boy,' Laura said, but she suddenly sounded strained. 'You can meet them yourself.'

'Should we wash up?' Kelly asked a bit too fast, not wanting to think about anyone needing support. A royal welcome… It was all very well eating toasted sandwiches but no one in this family would forget for long that they were royal. Including her?

And Rafael was shrugging. Moving on. He had no choice—he might as well move forward with good humour.

'If you think I'm meeting dignitaries plus doing the washing-up you have rocks in your head,' he retorted and managed a grin. 'There has to be some advantage of being royal. We can leave the washing-up to the staff.'

'I'm a failure as a mother,' Laura mourned.

'If you're starting to count my shortcomings then we'll walk you home,' Rafael told her, smiling across at Kelly. 'That is if you feel like a walk before bed. If you're like me, you'll still be thinking it's morning. My entire body clock is upside down.'

Hers, too. She'd slept in the plane. She felt wide awake.

She felt...

'I can walk myself home,' Laura said briskly. 'It's just past the gatehouse.'

'There are bogeymen out there,' Rafael said. 'The ghosts of a thousand royals.'

'And your father's one of them,' Laura retorted. 'You think any bogeyman would get me when your father's around to protect me?' She smiled fondly up at her son and caught his hand, letting him swing her to her feet. 'Rafael's father died here when Rafael was fifteen,' she told Kelly. 'It's why I've never wanted to leave. It still feels as if he's here.'

'You're just a romantic,' her son said.

'And you're not?'

'Absolutely not,' Rafael retorted. 'What about it, Kelly? Will you help escort my mother home, keeping her from bogeymen?'

'Are you staying with your mother?'

'No,' he said brusquely and Kelly thought he and his mother must have talked about this already. It seemed to have touched a nerve. 'My mother believes if I'm to do a decent job as Prince Regent then I live here. In the State Apartments.'

Kass's rooms. She'd never been admitted to them in the time she'd been here, but she'd walked past open doors. She'd never seen so much opulence in her life.

'You'll enjoy that,' she managed and he stared at her as if she'd lost her mind.

'Plenty of room for toys,' she ventured and his mother choked.

'There surely is. See, Rafael, there's a new way of looking at things.' She was walking towards the door. 'I don't need an escort, thank you, children, but…'

'But you're having an escort,' Rafael growled.

CHAPTER FIVE

So THEY walked Laura through the magnificent palace grounds, across the manicured lawns and past the extravagant fountains, down through the tiered rose gardens, brushing around the edge of the woodland area, following a path that was worn from years of royal tread. The moon was full. The woodland held night birds Kelly had never heard before, their calls eerie and wondrous in the moonlight. Nightingales? Maybe. She'd never heard a nightingale. She remembered feeling romantic all those years ago, wishing she'd hear one.

Romance was for the past. She was a sensible woman who'd learned her lesson.

She walked silently on the left of Laura. Rafael walked on her right, holding his mother's arm lightly.

He seemed protective, Kelly thought, and wondered why. Was there a reason he needed to protect her? She seemed a totally self-contained lady.

'So who gets to support Matty at the coronation?' Laura asked and there was a deathly silence.

'Coronation?' Kelly said cautiously.

'Uh-oh,' Rafael said.

'You knew it was coming,' his mother said. 'Didn't you?'

'Yes, but…'

'But you intended to be back in Manhattan. Not possible now. Not possible ever. You need to be part of it, Rafael.'

'Dress uniform,' he said with loathing.

'You like your dress sword,' Kelly said and he shook his head.

'I look ridiculous in a dress sword.'

'You look…' She hesitated.

'Magnificent is the word you're looking for,' Laura said fondly. 'His papa looked wonderful in dress regalia too.'

'And it did a lot for Papa,' Rafael said curtly. 'I suppose I have to be there.'

'Of course you do,' Laura told him. 'Crater's been organizing it while you've been away. You need to swear all sorts of things—basically whatever Matty would have to swear if he was old enough.'

'I think Kelly should do it,' Rafael said and Kelly winced.

'Hey, not me. I'm not royal material.'

'Neither of you sound committed,' Laura said cautiously.

Kelly said solidly, 'That's because I'm not.'

'You know, this country does need a royal presence,' Laura said. They'd reached the gate into the dower house and paused. The dower house was a miniature castle—exquisite. The garden here was a mass of wild flowers and shrubbery that seemed almost a wilderness. Kelly could smell jasmine and roses and…gardenia? Honeysuckle? The scene in the moonlight was fantastic.

But Laura wasn't focusing on gardens. She had a wider picture. 'This country's been let go,' Laura said, speaking earnestly to both of them. 'Neither Kass nor his father cared a toss about the country. Rafael, it nearly killed your father…'

'It did kill my father,' he said bitterly.

'A fall from a horse killed your father.'

'And then he wasn't permitted near the old Prince because disability made him nervous. So he couldn't do a thing.'

'Rafael's father tried to manage the economy of the place,' Laura explained to Kelly. 'He did what he could to make things easier for the people of Alp de Ciel. Then, when he was injured, his father, the old Prince, simply took all his royal duties from him.'

'Which pretty much killed him,' Rafael said. 'So why you'd think I'd want to pick up the pieces now…'

'Your father would want you to.'

'My father's dead,' Rafael said. 'I'm a toy-maker, Mama.'

'And a good one,' she said warmly and stood on tiptoe to kiss him. 'But the two aren't mutually exclusive. Prince of the blood and toy-maker on the side.'

'I'm a toy-maker,' he repeated. 'I'll do what I must here, and nothing more.'

'See, that's just the problem,' she said. Instead of opening the garden gate, she hitched herself up to sit on the drystone wall round the garden. She swung her legs against the stone and surveyed Kelly and Rafael with care.

'This country is a responsibility,' she said. 'A huge responsibility. And Matty's too little to take it on.'

'No one's taken it on for the last fifty years,' Rafael said.

'Your father tried to. It wasn't his job but…'

'You're right. It wasn't his job. It isn't mine.'

'It is,' she said forcibly. 'You're Prince Regent. The country needs you.'

'Don't you start,' he snapped. 'Kelly's already blackmailed me into staying.'

'Ah, yes,' Laura said softly. 'Kelly.'

'Hey, don't look at me,' Kelly said, startled. 'I'm not even royal.'

'I'm sorry, my dear, but that's where you're wrong,' Laura said sternly. 'You were royal from the minute you married Kass. You were even more royal the moment you bore him a son. This is your country.'

'It's not my country.'

'Someone has to take responsibility for it,' she said sadly. 'It's impoverished. Everyone knows that. The industries need a complete overhaul— the farming techniques are antiquated. There's money in the royal coffers to subsidise improvements, reform, but nothing's done. So far there's been little protest by the people. We have an extraordinarily accepting population. But now…'

'Now what?' Rafael said ominously and his

mother kicked the stone wall some more and looked from Rafael to Kelly and back again.

'Now there are three countries leading by example,' she said. 'Alp de Montez, Alp d'Estella and Alp d'Azuri. Three of the four principalities created all those centuries ago and almost destroyed by generation after generation of royalty who bled them dry with their own greed. Within the last few years each of these three countries have had their governments transformed. Each royal house has finally taken responsibility for their countries. They're now run as true democracies with an overarching sovereign. Their industries are thriving. Tourists are attracted in droves and the people here are looking at their neighbours and asking why not us?'

'They can do it,' Rafael said nervously.

'No, dear, *they* can't,' his mother said. '*They* being individuals within this country who want change. There's no avenue for change. The only way change is possible is with constitutional reform, and with enormous amounts of energy, commitment and sheer hard work by the incumbent sovereign. And, in case you hadn't noticed, that's you two.'

'Not me,' Kelly said,

'Not me, either,' Rafael said and his mother sighed.

'That's what Kass said.'

'Mama, I'm only here because Kelly forced me to be here,' Rafael growled. 'To take this all on…' He sounded bleak.

But there was a trace of acceptance in his voice, Kelly thought. There was more than a trace of his father in him. Despite his distaste for royalty, he'd agreed to meet this deputation tonight. She watched his face and thought yes, he'd do it. And it wasn't just her blackmail that was making him commit.

He was no Kass.

But was Laura asking her to share?

'I'm only here for my son,' she whispered.

'Do you think you can stay separate?' Laura asked gently.

'I think I don't know anything,' she whispered.

'You're a historian. You do the minimum amount of research on this place and you'll find out what I say is the truth.'

'So what do you want me to do about it?'

'I think you should both be royal,' Laura said gently and then, as Kelly stared at her in dismay, she shook her head, rueful.

'Rafael, you know it's what your father would have wanted. He hated what his father and his brother did to this country.'

'I hated what they did to him,' Rafael retorted.

'It's not the country's fault. Nor is what Kass did to you the country's fault, my dear,' she told Kelly. 'Do the research,' she ordered and swung herself off her wall and opened the gate. 'Make no promises yet. But think, my dears. Think, oh, think, of what the pair of you could achieve. Rafael, you're due to meet the country's representatives in half an hour. Kelly, if you could find it in you to help…'

'I can't.'

'Just think about it,' she demanded flatly, and disappeared into the house before either of them could reply.

Why had she come with Rafael and his mother, Kelly thought frantically as Laura disappeared. It meant she had to walk home alone with Rafael and he was making her nervous. He was big and silent and just…there.

He was as preoccupied as she was. Laura's words were echoing in the night air. So much to take on board…

They walked slowly through the woodland path towards the stables. The castle loomed before them, vast and majestic. The night was warm and filled with scents from the garden—a magic night.

'Is that a nightingale?' she asked before she could help herself and Rafael paused and listened and then shrugged.

'Yep. They're common.'

'Nightingales are common?'

'It's this whole damned fairy tale setting,' he said morosely. 'It does your head in. Like wearing a dress sword. I make toys. I don't want to live in make-believe any more than I have to.'

'I won't live in make-believe.'

'The problem is,' he said, 'it's not make-believe. It's real. Your son has to take over responsibility for this country and he's five years old.'

'My son needs to take over responsibility for this country in twenty years.'

'Meaning you're landing it fair in my corner.'

'Yes,' she said and walked on. Rafael stopped and stared at her.

'You could at least sound guilty,' he called and she turned and kept walking, but backwards so she could watch him in the moonlight.

'Why should I feel guilty?'

'If you hadn't had Matty I wouldn't be in this mess.'

'Yes, you would. Some other woman would have had the heir to the throne. Kass would still have died and you might have got someone who wasn't nicely determined to keep herself out of your way, out of trouble, out of sight.'

'So during the coronation…'

'I'll watch,' she conceded. 'I'll find myself a corner up the back.'

'You look ridiculous in baggy sweaters,' he said and she froze.

'I beg your pardon.'

'You're meant to be royal. You looked fantastic in crinoline and hoops.'

'And you look fantastic in your dress sword,' she said. 'But I was playing dress-ups for a reason that no longer exists. Your reasons keep going for another twenty years.'

'Kelly, help me here.'

'Help you do what?'

'We can do it together,' he said, pleading. 'You can take some of the pressure from me. If you'll play the princess…'

'No.'

'Kelly…'

'No!' She turned and stalked round the corner of the stables. And stopped.

Matty was walking towards them. He was in his pyjamas and bedroom slippers. He had his thumb in his mouth. He was walking determinedly towards the stables and he looked not even his full five years old.

'Matty,' she said and he looked up and saw them and froze.

'It's okay,' she said quickly. Rafael came round the corner of the stables and paused beside her. 'It's okay, Matty. It's only Rafael and me.'

'I want to see Blaze,' Matty whispered. He'd relaxed a little when he'd seen Rafael but he still sounded guilty.

'Blaze?'

'My papa's horse,' he said in a thread of a whisper. Then his voice firmed. 'Blaze is my horse now. I thought about him while I was in Australia. I thought and thought. Papa's dead. I don't think anyone's told Blaze.'

'I'm sure someone's already told him,' Kelly said. 'And we can tell him again in the morning. Sweetheart, you should be in bed.'

'I was in bed for hours and hours,' Matty said.

'I woke up and it feels like morning. So I had to tell Blaze.'

'Matty, Blaze already knows that your papa is dead,' Rafael said. They were standing side by side, looking down at the little prince. Matty was looking young, vulnerable but also determined. His small chin jutted forward in a gesture Kelly was starting to recognize.

'I should have told him myself,' Matty said fretfully. 'He's my horse.'

'I guess we need to come with you then, to make sure he's okay,' Rafael said. 'If it's okay with your mama.'

Horses. She didn't want to go anywhere near horses. Especially not Kass's horse. Blaze was the magnificent animal that had propelled her into trouble in the first place. She cast a despairing glance at Rafael but, to her astonishment, he took her hand and squeezed, almost as if he understood.

'A quick visit and then bed,' he said. 'Better than wasting time arguing. Matty, do you know where Blaze is stabled?'

'Of course I do,' Matty said scornfully.

'Then lead on,' Rafael said gently and the

little boy looked uncertainly up at the adults before him, then shrugged and led the way into the stables.

They were just as Kelly remembered.

Six years ago Kass had brought her in here at dawn, introduced her to each of the royal horses and then said, 'Choose your mount.'

For Kelly, who loved horses almost more than life itself, it had been the sexiest thing Kass could possibly have done. She'd walked between each stall while Kass had stood indulgently back, like a genie who'd just oozed from his bottle and snapped his fingers.

Then he'd called the stable-hands to saddle the mare of her choice; he'd mounted the huge black stallion with the blaze of white on its forehead and they'd ridden out into the dawn together.

It had been heady stuff for a kid who'd spent her life lusting after a horse of her own. Heady enough stuff to remove any sense of self-preservation, to make her walk straight into a web that she could never walk out of.

Now she walked into the stables feeling just the same—as if a door would slam behind her and she'd be stuck. But Matty was walking steadily forward to the first stall.

Kelly peered nervously over the door. A mare stood placidly at the rear of the stall, head down in the manger.

'It's not Blaze.'

'He's here somewhere. I have to find him.'

'He's at the end,' Rafael said and motioned along the doorways. His height gave him the advantage. Kelly turned and saw what Rafael was seeing, the great stallion standing at ease, staring out at them with seeming unconcern.

She flinched and Rafael stepped forward and took her arm.

'It's okay.'

'I know it's okay,' she muttered. 'I…I know horses.'

'Do you know Blaze?' Matty asked.

'I've met him,' she muttered. 'Matty, he's too big for you to go near.'

'He's my horse,' Matty said, sounding rebellious. 'My papa said the Prince has to have the best, and Blaze is the best. I knew when he died I'd have to take care of him. Like the country. Crater says I have to take care of the country.'

It was such an astounding statement coming out of the mouth of a five-year-old that neither Rafael nor Kelly could think of a response.

'But Crater says you'll help,' Matty said, almost indulgently, and walked forward to Blaze's stall. He stood looking uncertainly up at the big horse, as if unsure how to approach him. 'He's very big.'

'I think your father would want you to ride a much smaller horse for a while,' Kelly said but Matty shook his head.

'Someone has to ride Blaze.'

'Maybe Rafael…'

'I don't ride,' Rafael said.

'Me either,' Kelly retorted.

'Crater said my mother rides like the wind,' Matty said, turning to stare at her as if he'd been given deeply erroneous information—information that was very, very important.

'People change,' Kelly said. 'I…I don't ride any more.'

'Why not?'

'I just don't,' she said helplessly. 'I study instead.'

'Who will help me look after the horses?'

'I…we'll employ people,' Kelly said. 'Maybe…I mean we probably already do. Don't we, Rafael?'

'I guess.' Rafael peered hopefully into the stalls. 'They've all got hay and fresh water. They're obviously being taken care of.'

'But I need to know for sure,' Matty said definitely. 'I'll find out tomorrow. And Ellen says there's a dep…a deputation coming from the village. I need to see them.'

'They're coming tonight and they're coming to see your Uncle Rafael,' Kelly told him.

'I'm the Prince,' Matty said. 'Uncle Rafael doesn't want to be the Prince.'

'Uncle Rafael is the Prince until you're older,' Kelly said.

'He doesn't even want to ride horses.'

'He doesn't have a choice,' Kelly snapped. It was too much. Her tiny prince was looking cold and shaky. She picked him up before he could make a protest and held him close. 'Meanwhile, you need to go back to bed. Stop worrying about tomorrow.'

'I have to worry about it,' Matty said. 'I'm…'

'You're a little boy who needs to be a little boy,' she said solidly. 'And little boys need to do what their mothers tell them. Which is go to bed and not worry. Your Uncle Rafael will take care of everything.'

'Sure,' Rafael said morosely.

'See,' Matty said. 'He doesn't want to.'

'I do want to,' Rafael said. 'I meant to say *sure*.

As in happy sure. It's just because I have jet lag that it came out grumpy.'

'You're sure?'

'I'm sure,' he said and beamed. Kelly almost laughed. It was some crazy beam. It was a Cheshire cat beam, ridiculous in its insincerity.

But it seemed to do the trick. Matty relaxed into her arms and snuggled against her.

'I just thought…I worried about Blaze. And the villagers… They used to come to see Papa when he was alive. Papa called them fools but Ellen said if Papa was a proper prince he'd listen to what they need and do something about it. I want to be a proper prince.'

'You will be,' Kelly said unsteadily. 'Later. Not now. Not until you're almost as high as Blaze.'

'Uncle Rafael will take care of everything?'

'Uncle Rafael will take care of everything,' she said. 'Now, I'm taking you back to bed.'

She tucked him into bed, and stayed with him until he was asleep. She decided she ought to go to bed herself, but when she looked out of the nursery window she saw Rafael.

He was sitting on one of the garden seats, staring out towards the Alps beyond. He was dressed in his royal regalia again. She wasn't sure about the sword, but she could see braid on his shoulders.

A prince waiting to meet the townspeople.

What had he said?

'We can do it together. You can take some of the pressure from me. If you'll play the princess...'

She wasn't about to play the princess. Once she had. Never again.

She should close the curtains.

She couldn't.

Rafael had been asked to take on what she couldn't. She couldn't let him off the hook, but that didn't stop her feeling guilty.

Matty was solidly asleep again. Marguerite was right next door. And Rafael looked...alone.

She glanced down at her clothing—jeans and baggy sweater.

It was hardly princess wear.

That was okay.

Not okay if she wanted to help.

Could she help?

Maybe she could, she thought. Just a little. After all, Rafael was in a relationship with his Anna. He was no threat to her. To hide up here like a hermit... Maybe it was even silly.

But what to wear…

She bit her lip.

'Go on, Kelly,' she told herself, whispering into the night. 'You've been playing dress-ups for five years now. Maybe you can play dress-ups a little bit longer.'

Her rooms were just as she'd left them. Kelly turned the handle of the vast oak doors leading into the suite she'd stayed in five years ago and the sight of the dressing gown on the side table made her frown again. Why hadn't it been thrown out?

But then… This suite was one of many and it was as far from Kass's apartments as it was possible to be. If Kass had brought guests—women—here he'd want them a lot closer. For the staff to destroy her possessions would have taken a direct order and Kass must simply never have given the order.

The crib that had stood beside the bed for those few short weeks had gone. Otherwise it was exactly as she'd left it. Cleaned and cared for and ready for her to come home.

She wasn't home. She had no place here.

Not true. She was Matty's mother. And maybe it wouldn't hurt to help.

She was being silly. Dumb. But just on the off chance…

She walked across to the vast bank of wardrobes and slid back the doors. And found what she'd half expected.

Here was her wardrobe. A wardrobe fit for a princess.

The first few weeks with Kass had been dream-like. A royal fantasy. She'd been whisked to Paris, she'd been showered with every luxury, she'd been wooed with every one of Kass's several charms.

He'd taken her shopping. Not the shopping normal people did, but shopping where he'd take her into the most expensive boutiques he could find, introduced her grandly as Kellyn, Princess of Alp de Ciel, settled himself into a settee, called for a drink and watched as she tried on one outfit after another.

For Kelly, who'd thought the epitome of fashion was her little red dress, it had been an eye-opener. For a while she'd thought it was fantastic.

And these were the legacy, left behind as Kass had forced her to leave. One designer gown after another. Dresses that had been so expensive their price tags had made her eyes water.

Ridiculous dresses.

She was here for a purpose. She had to do it fast or she'd lose courage.

She tugged a dress from the racks—an elegant black cocktail frock, tiny capped sleeves, a sweetheart neckline, a hemline that was too long for Kass's taste but which the boutique owner had gasped over.

'Oh, Your Highness, it makes you look just like Audrey Hepburn.'

Hardly, Kelly thought, but she grinned and held it up in front of her. She was the same size as six years ago. It wouldn't hurt to dress up just a little.

Her shoes were still here. All her shoes. What about her jewellery?

Was she being really, really dumb? she demanded of herself as she pulled out the top drawer of her bureau.

Maybe she was, but Rafael was waiting.

The men were angry and impatient and barely civil. Rafael didn't blame them. Their needs were urgent and they'd been ignored for too long.

'We need to sit down and look at the whole situation,' he said, but that was just what they didn't want to hear.

'You're just like your cousin,' one of the men snapped. 'He didn't care and neither do you. Do you realise the threat to the village…?'

'He doesn't realise it yet, but he will,' a soft voice said from the doorway. 'We both will.'

Rafael turned—and gasped.

He'd brought the men into the first of the salons just by the grand entrance. The room was vast and ornate, with magnificent settees gathered around a fireplace that was truly awesome. But outside in the entrance there were marble columns, a chandelier with so many crystals it must take an army to clean it, a truly magnificent entry.

Kelly was framed against it. A slip of a girl in a dress that was the epitome of elegance. It hugged her figure, showing off every lovely curve. Her hair was swept up into a knot that might be casual—wisps of curls were escaping—but it accentuated the simplicity of her dress. Her legs looked long and elegant, her black sandals made her feet look sooo sexy…

The whole outfit made her look sooo sexy. The eight men in the deputation were rising to their feet as one and Rafael did too.

'I'm so sorry I'm late,' Kelly was murmuring

as she crossed to Rafael's side. 'My son is a little unsettled after the flight and I needed to make sure he was asleep before I left.'

'Princess...Kellyn?' someone breathed and Rafael caught his breath and made the introductions.

Her outfit was brilliant, he thought as he watched the men's reactions. She'd been described to the country as a slut. This outfit made her look anything but.

She rested her hand lightly on his arm. It wasn't a proprietorial gesture. It was a gesture of solidarity.

'You do need to give us a little time,' she said softly, glancing up at Rafael and smiling, as if this was something they'd discussed in depth. 'My husband has just died, and Prince Rafael has only just been able to bring me back here. Yes, there's been major damage done to the country by royal neglect. But injustice has been done to Rafael and to me, as well as to you, his people. Prince Kass forbade me access to my son. He refused to allow Prince Rafael or his father before him to assist you. These great injustices can now be reversed. I understand your anger. Rafael and I share that anger and we intend to do everything we can to redress the situation.'

It was brilliant, Rafael thought, stunned. In one fell swoop she'd deflected the anger, by linking herself to him, by acting as if they were a team. Yes, these people were furious that their country had been neglected, but this slip of a girl had been kicked out of the country and denied her child.

'We thought you…we thought…'

'There have been many lies spread about the Princess Kellyn,' Rafael said strongly. 'Those lies need to be redressed. As many things in this country need to be redressed. You people are from the village. What I want from you is a list of your immediate concerns and your suggestions as to what can be done to address them. Can you get that to me as soon as you can? I need to go further— get things moving throughout the whole country— but of course you people are our neighbours and maybe your concerns have to take priority.'

'When will you be leaving again?' one of the men asked, but the belligerence had gone out of his voice. He was clearly unsure.

'I won't be,' Rafael said, and his voice was clear and calm and sure. He put a hand over Kelly's. If she was to help…

If she was to stand by his side…anything was possible, he thought. The bleakness that had been with him since he'd heard of Kass's death lifted for the first time. These people needed his help. He could do this.

'There will be occasional trips abroad,' he said, and it was a struggle now not to let this strange sense of exultation enter his voice. 'Made out of necessity. I know there was anger that I left last week, so soon, but my priority was to restore Princess Kellyn to her rightful place. Now that's been done, both of us will be based here. Ready to listen to what you need of us.'

'My role is mother to Prince Mathieu,' Kelly said, suddenly sounding nervous. 'You understand that my brief marriage to Kass hasn't fitted me for any other role. But I'll be supporting Prince Rafael in the background.'

There was a murmur of approval. And sympathy. And… excitement?

'We understand it will take time for you both to find your feet here,' one of the men—the leader—said at last. He moved forward to shake Rafael's hand. 'We've heard enough tonight to content us. We'll make this list and we'll get it to you as soon as possible. And we look forward to working with you.' He glanced across at Kelly. 'With both of you.'

They walked out into the grand entrance, to the huge sweep of carved steps, to see the deputation off. The men climbed into their several cars and departed. Rafael and Kelly stood side by side until they were out of sight.

'Thank you,' Rafael said softly as the sound of the cars faded. 'You saved my hide. They were all ready for a spot of anarchy.' He moved away a little so he could see her. 'Wow,' he said softly. 'Wow and wow and wow. You took their breath away. You took my breath away.' He frowned. 'But I thought you didn't bring a dress.'

'It's part of my past,' she said. 'It seems I still have a wardrobe of dresses here. Mostly chosen by Kass.'

'Kass never chose that.'

'No.' She ran her hands self-consciously along her sides and the luxurious silk felt smooth and lovely under her hands. 'I chose this.'

'You like clothes,' he said on a note of discovery.

'For my pains. I try not to.'

'Don't try,' he said urgently. 'You're beautiful. The people will love you.'

'You're saying I should wear the clothes Kass chose for me?'

'Of course I'm not. You could come to Manhattan with me,' he said. 'When we get this place sorted. Money's not an issue—the royal coffers have an amount set aside that is purely for personal maintenance of the immediate royal family. That's us. It's enough to make you think that maybe buying a lottery ticket might be a waste of time. You and Matty could take a few days and come play on Fifth Avenue.' He grinned and looked her up and down, his smile enough to make her blush—really blush. 'Matty and I would love to watch you enjoy yourself setting yourself up for your new life here.'

'What about Anna?' she asked curiously, trying to get her colour under control. 'Isn't she due here?'

'She should be here tomorrow,' Rafael said. 'I've organized the stuff from my development workshop to be freighted over and she's super-vising. But don't worry about Anna. Any shopping we're organising, she'll have her hand up before me.'

'Oh.' She wasn't quite sure what was happening here. The appreciation in his eyes was warm and intimate. Yet he spoke about Anna with matter-of-fact directness.

'Why aren't you in your attic?' he asked, cutting across her train of thought.

'I saw you out here.' She hesitated. 'I felt...I don't know. Maybe if I can help I will. Just occasionally,' she added hastily as she saw the leap of hope in his eyes. 'Not on a regular basis.' She bit her lip. 'I...maybe I've been a bit mean. I am grateful to you. For Matty,' she said softly. 'I do need to thank everyone here. You've all done a lovely job of bringing him up. He's a darling.'

'And so responsible,' Rafael said.

'He doesn't need to be responsible.'

'As long as I'm responsible. Or you're responsible. And look at us. We even look like royals.'

'I'm play-acting,' she said, 'to help out. I'm going back to my attic tomorrow.'

'That's a damned waste.'

'It shouldn't be.'

'You don't need me.'

'No?'

For a long moment he stared at her as if she'd just asked a question that was really dumb. She gazed back at him, bewildered. But then...

But then things started clicking into place.

It had been five years since any man had looked at her like Rafael was looking at her, but she knew the signs. He was staring at her as if he were hungry. As if she were…

Desirable?

'No,' she said and held up her hands as if in defence.

'It's all very well to say no,' Rafael snapped, stepping towards her so fast he was suddenly way too close. 'It's the last thing I want. Or it should be the last thing I want.'

'What?' she said, confused.

'You,' he said and the world stood still again.

'I…don't,' she said at last, somehow taking a step back, and he shook his head as if trying to clear a fog.

'Yeah. Maybe I'm being dumb. Go to bed, Kelly.'

'You're sending me to bed?'

'I'm sending you away,' he said, exasperated. 'I need you to go away.'

'Like Kass.'

'No!' And, before she knew what he was about, he'd seized her hands and tugged her close. 'That's just it. Don't you see—I'm not the least like Kass. Kass represented everything about this

place that I hate. Royalty. The perfection of it…
Do you know my father was thrown from his
horse and maimed? He was crippled but as well
as that he had a massive scar running down the
side of his face. He lost the sight of one eye.
Until then, he'd worked like a navvy in this
place—that the Principality hasn't bankrupted
itself until now is solely down to my father's
economic acumen and the fact that the old prince
never bothered to interfere. But as soon as my
father was injured he wasn't permitted any part
of the running of the place. He was simply struck
off. It just killed him—his injuries, but more—
the fact that he was useless. My mother and I
could do nothing. And here I am, being useful
again. Useful. And here you are and you're
Kass's bride…'

'Hey…'

'And the last thing I want is to feel sorry for
you,' he said. 'And I don't and that's just the
trouble. Sympathy is something I could deal
with. But you're standing here looking so
damned sexy it's melting the soles of my boots,
and the way I feel…I just…'

'You just?' She was trying to pull away but he
was having none of it.

'I just,' he said and he tugged her tight against him.

And he kissed her.

The shock made her freeze.

For the first couple of seconds—those vital seconds when she should have pulled away, before his mouth even touched hers—shock didn't let her move. His hands were holding hers with a warmth and a strength that locked her to him. She'd been tugging back—sort of—but not with real desperation. But now…

His hands tugged her tight and his mouth lowered on to hers. In shock she looked up at him, and then his lips claimed hers and it was a done deal. She was being kissed, whether she willed it or not.

Rafael…

He felt…He felt…

She stopped trying to figure what he felt. She stopped trying to figure what she felt. She just…was.

She hadn't touched a man for six years. She'd sworn to never…

So much for swearing, for there was no way any mere resolution could get in the way of this.

Her mouth met his, merged, and her body simply went into meltdown. She had no will to do anything but simply be—to let him take her as he willed, to let his hands create their magic, to let the sensations sweeping over her take their course, transform her as they willed, lift her out of her dreary yesterdays and turn her into a woman desired.

For that was what she was. There was no mistaking the urgency of how he felt about her. His hands had her firmly round the waist, tugging her into him so her breasts were flattened against his chest. She could feel his heart beating under hers. She opened her lips and felt his tongue begin a slow, delicious plunder that would have made her moan in pleasure if in doing so she might not have risked breaking the moment.

She was risking nothing. She was doing her own holding, taking what she needed from this man, soaking in the warmth and strength and arrant male desire.

It had been too long. Far too long.

Rafael…

She was kissing him back, as fiercely as he was kissing her, taking as well as giving, quenching her own desperate needs.

Needs she'd told herself didn't exist.

Only, of course, they did. Six long years of nothing. Isolation and loneliness and betrayal.

Rafael…

The kiss went on and on. Neither wanted it to end. Neither could conceive of it ending. The night was still and warm. There was no movement in the forecourt—the castle staff had long gone to bed. There was only this man and this woman, taking what they both desperately needed.

And when the kiss finally ended, as even the best kiss must inevitably do, Kelly took a step back and put her fingers to her lips and knew that her world had changed.

'N…no,' she whispered and she saw her own shock mirrored in Rafael's eyes.

'No,' he agreed, sounding as if he didn't know what the word meant.

'I didn't want to kiss you,' she whispered.

'You're Kass's woman,' he said blankly and that brought reality crashing back around the pair of them.

Kass's woman…

The feeling of unreality dissipated. Here and now crashed right back.

'How dare you?'

'I don't dare,' he said. 'That was dumb.'

She stared at him, confounded. The kiss had been dumb. Of course it had been dumb. But to say it…

'Don't you touch me,' she stammered and the confusion in his eyes faded.

'You don't want it?'

'Of course not.'

'Of course not. We're birds of a feather, Kelly. We want nothing to do with this.'

'But it's not this we're talking about,' she managed. 'Not royalty. Not now. No, I don't want any more contact than I'm forced to have with royalty to be a good mother to Matty. But as far as kissing you…'

'You looked at me,' he said as if that explained everything and she glared.

'So you're saying I goaded you into it. Like wearing red patent shoes.'

'Pardon?' he said, startled.

'You don't wear red patent shoes,' she said patiently. 'Everyone knows they incite the senses and reflect your knickers.'

'Really?'

'Not that it has anything to do with the here and now,' she said, fighting to get a grip. 'And I should never have worn this dress. When's Anna coming?'

'I told you. Tomorrow.'

'Then starting tomorrow, let's get this on a sensible footing,' she snapped. 'You and me... we see each other in terms of official duties. That's all.'

'That's all I want, too.'

'Because, of course, I'm Kass's woman.'

'I didn't mean to say that.'

'You did say it,' she snapped. 'And it hurt. I was dumb enough to fall for a good royal come-on, and if you think I'd be dumb enough to fall twice...Kass's woman or not...you'd be out of your mind. So you needn't look at me as if I'm trying to jump you or, heaven forbid, put another wedding ring on my finger...'

'I'm not.'

'Because I'm not,' she snapped, refusing to let him interrupt. 'I'm going to bed.'

'Good.'

'And Kass's...the royal suite is round the far side of the castle,' she said. 'As far from my attics as it's possible to get. And I can lock my doors.'

'Kelly, I'm not trying to seduce you.'

'You kissed me and that's enough. More than enough. I don't even want a handshake from a prince of the blood.'

'I'm not…'

'A prince of the blood. Yes, you are.'

'As you're Kass's bride,' Rafael said, sounding goaded. 'Princess Royal. You represent everything I don't want about this place.'

'Well, it's good we have that cleared up,' she snapped. 'Just so we're clear. You dragged me back here and now you tell me I'm part of your problem. Sorry, Rafael, I have problems of my own to sort.'

She should stalk away. She should just turn and leave. Instead, she stood in the moonlight and watched him try to think of something else to say—something that would make sense of this crazy situation they'd landed in.

He couldn't. He didn't. And finally there was no choice. She turned away. 'Goodnight,' she said stiffly.

'Kelly?'

She didn't turn round. She simply stood still and waited for him to say what he needed to say.

'I'm sorry,' he said at last. 'That should never have happened. It won't happen again. I promise.'

'Just as well,' she muttered.

And went to bed.

* * *

But not to sleep.

What had she been thinking of—to let him kiss her and to kiss him back?

It was because he was…gorgeous?

Rafael de Boutaine, Prince Regent of Alp de Ciel. He'd kissed her senseless.

As Kass had.

No. He was as different from Kass as it was possible to be. Kelly lay in the lovely double bed Rafael had organized to be delivered into her attic room and watched the moonbeams play on the ceiling. She shouldn't have the new bed, she thought. She wanted to be like a forgotten relation, left to penury while on the other side of the castle, on the royal side, Rafael swanned round in luxury, enjoying his magnificent suite of rooms, being…Prince Regent.

'I'd hate it,' she muttered.

She didn't hate Rafael. She'd loved it tonight, she conceded. She'd loved feeling beautiful. She'd loved standing side by side with Rafael while he'd organized affairs of state. She'd loved the way he'd gasped as she'd walked into the room. And the way the warmth had stayed in his eyes.

In fact, the way she was feeling about Rafael…

had to be suppressed. The part of her that had been wounded to the core five years ago clenched into horror.

To fall in love with another prince…

What was she thinking? How could she be falling in love? Just because the man had kissed her…

'The man's seriously fabulous,' she told the ceiling and closed her eyes, as if she could block out the thought of him.

His partner would be here tomorrow—a woman called Anna. They'd get on with the ruling Laura told them was needed and she'd retire to her books. For the next twenty years.

'Which is what I want,' she whispered into the dark, 'isn't it?'

'Yes,' her mind screamed but there was a tiny part of her that was stubbornly refusing to agree.

Why had he kissed her? Did he have no sense at all?

Yes, he'd agreed to take on the Regency, but that was as far as it went. He didn't want to get any more fond of Matty than he already was, and he sure as hell didn't want to get any more fond of Matty's mother.

But he'd kissed her.

The thought shocked him. He hadn't known what he intended to do until it happened and then…then it was too late. It was lucky that Kelly had sense for the pair of them.

It's like quicksand, he thought savagely, the royal quagmire hauling him in.

He thought back to the days after his father's accident. Up until then, Rafael had been cool with being royal. Kass, his older cousin, had been an arrogant, egotistical bore. Worried about the influence Kass might have, his parents had sent Rafael to boarding school. He'd thoroughly enjoyed it, but he'd loved coming back in the holidays. He'd lived on horseback, roaming this beautiful little country with an ever-growing appreciation.

But then his father had been injured, and over the course of one summer life had changed. Kass and his father had simply cut off the brother and uncle who'd once been useful to them, but whose use-by date had been the moment he'd become uncomfortable to look at.

The last time he'd come outside… It had been just before Rafael was due to go back to school. Laura had convinced her husband to get some sun, so she and Rafael had pushed him into the garden.

Kass had walked past and had stopped dead.

'He's not to stay here,' he'd said harshly, speaking to Laura and not directly to his uncle. 'It upsets the staff. It makes me feel sick. He's not to come within sight of the castle.'

That one vicious order had been enough to make Rafael's father return to the house. He'd died two months later, without having set foot in the garden again.

Rafael had made that vow as well. There was no way he ever intended to be of use to royalty. He wouldn't set foot in the castle. He'd hoped his mother would move. She hadn't and their access to each other had become confined to Laura's visits to the States.

And now, like it or not, here he was—of use to royalty as his father had once been of use to the old Prince and to Kass. It made him feel ill.

And tonight he'd kissed Kass's wife.

Why?

It was a web, he thought, a fine, gossamer web drawing him in tighter and tighter. Conscience and duty had him stuck here.

Like Kelly was stuck.

She wasn't stuck, he thought savagely. She could stay up in her attic and be an academic and not do anything, not be a part of it. Or do as she'd done tonight, emerge from her attic for a moment and then retreat the moment things got intense.

So why had he kissed her?

'Because I'm a fool,' he told the darkness and he rolled over in the royal bed and thought he could roll over six or seven times and not reach the edge.

'It's ludicrous.

'It's life as you'll know it for the next twenty years,' he said grimly. 'So get used to it. And keep your hands off that woman!'

CHAPTER SIX

KELLY woke to the sound of shouting in the fore-court. For a moment she couldn't remember where she was—the strange bed and the thick stone walls and narrow casement windows confused her. Then, as the events of the last few days flooded back, her bedroom door was flung open and Matty launched himself across her bed.

'Uncle Rafael's toys are here,' he said. 'Mama, come and see. Come and see.'

'I don't…'

'You have to come,' he said before she could protest. 'There's pancakes for breakfast and Cook's made heaps and heaps 'cos the truck drivers have come all the way from the border this morning and Anna's here and she's really crabby and I'll sit on your bed and wait for you to get dressed.'

She stared at her little son, helpless in the face of his enthusiasm. How could she tell him she'd been thinking of putting a little kitchenette up here, so that she didn't have to go down to the royal kitchens?

What sort of mother would say that?

He wanted her to come.

She peered through the casement. Men were unloading vast crates, carrying them into the main entrance.

'Where's Rafael?'

'He's in the dungeons,' Matty said with relish, as if the dungeons were truly gruesome. 'Cook said once upon a time there were ghosts in our dungeons with clanking chains, but Uncle Rafael said that the best way to get rid of ghosts is to bury them with sawdust. He's working already. Anna says he's burying his head in the sand but I think he's burying it in sawdust.'

'Well,' Kelly said cautiously, digesting this with care. She'd spent a lot of time figuring things out before she'd gone to sleep. Rafael had kissed her. Rafael was a de Boutaine. The man was obviously a womaniser, just like Kass.

She could deal with this situation, she thought. Disdain—that was the way to go. And distance.

'Maybe if Rafael's working I can come down to breakfast.'

'And then come to the stables?' Matty pleaded. 'Will you come riding?'

'I don't ride,' she said flatly. She pushed back her bedcovers. The silk dress was draped over the bedside chair. She pushed it back so it fell on to the floor behind, out of sight. 'Sorry, Matty, but that's an absolute.'

It was like a vast family. The huge kitchen was filled with people and noise and food.

For Kelly, whose only experience at the castle was silence, fear and formality, the sight that met her eyes as she walked into the kitchen was almost astonishing.

There was a big, buxom woman flipping pancakes in the world's biggest frying-pan on the vast electric range. There were two younger girls, one stirring what seemed to be a vat of batter, the other peeling a mound of potatoes a foot high. The men Kelly had seen carting the crates were seated at one end of the table, wrapping themselves round mounds of the pancakes, looking as if all their Christmases had come at once. Laura was there, talking to a man Kelly recognized as Crater. Crater. The sight of him made her flinch. She hadn't seen him since she'd arrived yesterday.

There was a younger woman as well—tall, almost statuesque, looking svelte in cream linen trousers and a lovely Aran pullover. Her blonde hair was piled high in an elegantly casual knot, she wore fabulous, dangling silver earrings and she looked amazing.

Kelly recognized her from the photograph she'd seen on the Internet—Anna.

'I've brought Mama down to breakfast,' Matty said in his clear voice, and everyone in the kitchen turned and looked at her. Kelly wanted to run.

But Matty had her hand and was tugging her forward. 'I said we were having pancakes so she came,' he said and Crater rose from his seat next to Laura and came round the table with his hand outstretched in welcome.

'Princess Kellyn. Your Highness.'

'Kelly,' she whispered, and dropped Matty's hand and backed instinctively away. The last time she'd talked to this man he'd been talking through the impossibility of her ever seeing her son again. She couldn't bear it.

'I need to apologise,' the elderly man said softly, but Anna was suddenly there, standing beside Crater, looking belligerent.

'Hell, no,' she said. 'Don't apologise to this woman. She's stuffed my life.'

'Hey,' Rafael said from the doorway behind her. He'd come in behind her without her hearing. 'She's stuffed whose life?'

'Everyone's,' Anna said. 'Every single one of our kids.'

'Whose kids?' Kelly asked blankly.

'Twenty kids thinking he's their hero,' Anna said bitterly. 'Twenty kids…'

'Who now need to swap their allegiance to you,' Rafael told her.

'I don't do kids,' Anna said flatly. 'I run a business. A business, Rafael, not a damned charity. Here you are, hauling the personal stuff over here, and if you think…'

'I absolutely think,' Rafael said and put his arms round her and hugged her.

But Anna hadn't finished with her grievance yet. She swiped his hands away and glowered. 'Don't you try your sweet-talk on me. Richard's having all sorts of fits—he didn't even want me to come now. And how the hell Kelly got you here…'

'I don't think I know what's going on,' Kelly said.

'That's because you haven't had breakfast,' Laura said calmly, rising from the table and handing her a warmed plate. 'Wrap yourself round some pancakes.'

'Then you can come down and see what I have in my dungeons. Meanwhile, we need to stop Anna being mean to you,' Rafael said. 'Come on, Anna, you can handle it. It's not like I had any choice.'

'Because of Kelly.' Anna glowered. 'You said you'd just need to spend a little time here for ceremonial duties, that all you had to do was persuade Kellyn to take over her rightful role and you could fade into the background again. Someone take that woman's pancakes away from her.'

'Not on your life,' Kelly said, concentrating on the only thing she could understand. Cook was ladling a stack of hot pancakes on to her plate and they smelled extraordinary. She didn't have a clue what was happening between Rafael and Anna, but guilt was hovering, ready to pounce.

She didn't have to accept it. She didn't have to find out what Anna was talking about, she told herself. Rafael's life was none of her business. She sat at the far end of the table, one of the truckers handed her a jug of maple syrup and she got down to business.

'I knew you'd like pancakes,' Matty said, pleased, and she smiled at his pleasure. This was her business—making her son smile.

The kitchen felt great, she thought as she ate. It was big and warm and friendly. She didn't feel out of place back in her jeans and baggy sweater. Even Anna's hostility seemed not particularly hostile—more resigned.

It was none of her business but some things seemed impossible. Maybe she could just ask…

'So you two have twenty children?' she ventured cautiously, and Rafael choked.

'Right. You see what you've done?'

'They might as well be your kids,' Anna retorted, unabashed. 'For all the trouble you've put into them.'

'I don't have twenty kids,' Rafael said. 'I have a sheltered workshop which employs twenty disabled young men and women.'

'Who are currently ready to hate the Princess Kellyn of Alp de Ciel,' Anna said. 'Because you've taken away their precious Rafael.'

'Oh,' Kelly said in a small voice.

'He had to come away anyway,' Laura said.

'Not all the time, he didn't,' Anna said. 'When Kass died he said he might have to spend a bit more time here. Not all the time.'

'So it's my fault,' Kelly said.

'Yes,' Anna retorted. Kelly thought about it. Rafael was looking at her as if he was quite happy for her to take the blame. How unfair was that?

'You'd think someone could have told me,' she said bluntly and fixed him with a look that put the blame right back where it belonged.

He didn't look the least bit guilty. He grinned. His grin made her feel warm from the toes up.

Ridiculous!

'You didn't tell her?' Anna demanded, turning back to Rafael.

'What was I supposed to tell her?' Rafael asked.

'How I'm dependent on you.'

'I told Kelly I had a partner.'

'Just not twenty kids.'

'It seemed a bit over-dramatic.'

'Rafael makes toys,' Laura said, taking pity on Kelly's confusion. 'Rafael has the most wonderful sheltered workshop in the world. He's built it up from one tiny idea, and now they export all over the world.'

'Robo-Craft,' Kelly said. 'He did tell me that.'

She frowned. So what hadn't he told her? Her ultimatum had real repercussions, not just for Rafael? She set down her knife and fork, her appetite suddenly gone.

'It's not like I'm closing down,' Rafael told her quickly. 'I'm just moving development here. Production will stay in Manhattan, overseen by Anna.'

'Who keeps trying to run the business like a business,' Anna said, sighing theatrically. 'Only production's dropped already, as everyone loves Rafael.'

'And now they have to learn to love Anna,' Rafael said. 'And they will.'

'So…' Kelly swallowed. There was a lot here to think about and she didn't know whether she had it right yet. 'So when I said you had to stay here…'

'Then I had to reorganize my business,' Rafael said. 'Which I've done.'

'And Anna's your…?'

'Business partner,' Anna said bluntly. 'More fool me. I'm an accountant.'

'Not your…partner-partner?'

'No,' Anna said, astonished. 'Why would you think that? I'd have brained him ten years ago if he was my partner-partner. Any sane woman would. Now my Richard—who is my partner-partner—is threatening to brain him for me.'

'Oh,' Kelly said. She was starting to feel wobbly.

Last night had seemed fraught. Dangerous. But last night she'd thought Rafael was messing around, being a typical de Boutaine, because Rafael had a partner.

This morning she'd discovered that Anna was his business partner. And she'd discovered more. That Rafael had some truly noble motives in there among his de Boutaine blood.

Last night she'd thought Rafael was sexy but a de Boutaine.

Now…now she just thought he was sexy. Clever. Skilled. Kind.

Unattached.

Very, very sexy.

She suddenly felt really, really exposed. The kitchen was too warm. It was almost claustrophobic.

She pushed her pancakes away.

'Is something wrong?' Laura asked, watching her with concern.

'I didn't want to blackmail anyone to come here.'

'If you did, we're very grateful to you,' Crater

said, smiling on her with approval. 'We need Rafael to run this principality. Someone has to take on the Crown.'

'But that's me,' Matty piped up. 'You said I'm the Crown Prince. This country is my res… responsibility.'

'Which Rafael will take care of for you until you're of age,' Crater told him gravely.

'You said I have to look after my people. I am the Prince.'

It silenced them all—this wisp of a child calmly accepting a burden that Rafael and Kelly would do anything to avoid.

Kelly stared down at her half-eaten pancakes, gulped and hauled the plate back in front of her. Maybe she couldn't bolt to her garret quite yet. But the pancakes didn't taste as good.

'You've taught Matty his royal duties?' Rafael asked Crater.

Crater nodded unhappily. 'He's had lessons.'

'Not from his father.'

'No. But Kass has hardly been here. I've taken it upon myself…'

'To load Matty with the burden of the Crown.'

'There was hardly a choice,' Crater said. 'I could never have predicted what's happened.

This country's desperate for leadership. Thankfully, now it's up to you.'

Oh, help, Kelly thought.

Until now she'd hardly seen Rafael, she thought bleakly. Or she had seen him but she'd seen a de Boutaine.

Now, he stood alone, a big man, loose-limbed, dressed in casual trousers, an open-necked shirt with sleeves rolled up to his elbows, a streak of grease on his forehead.

He looked vulnerable, she thought suddenly. He looked as if he were backed into a corner he hated.

She could retire to her garret when she wished. He couldn't.

'You don't have to worry.' Matty was clearly trying hard to understand what was going on. He came to his big cousin's side and slipped his hand into Rafael's before Rafael could guess what he intended. 'You can make your toys and I'll be the Prince. My mama will help me be the Prince.'

'Your mama intends to stay in her attic and read her books.'

'You might persuade her to come out a bit,' Anna said, enthusiastic again. 'For long enough to let Rafael come back to Manhattan and make his kids happy from time to time.'

'My life's here,' Rafael said, sounding as if it were a life sentence.

'But you will help,' Matty said to Kelly and she swallowed.

'I…of course. When I can.'

But she was suddenly much more unsure than she had been last night. Dressing up last night had seemed…well, even a little bit of fun. But to go any further, and to do it by Rafael's side when…when Anna wasn't his partner…

'I want you to ride with me,' Matty said and her heart closed—snap—like a clam closing on expected pain.

'Matty, I can't.'

'You can't ride?'

'I don't want to.'

'There's lots of that about,' Laura said sadly, standing and starting to clear plates. 'Let's just take each day as it comes. Starting now. We'll get these trucks unpacked and that'll make Rafael happy. He'll have his dungeons to play in.'

'And Mama will stay in her attic,' Matty said. 'Aunt Laura, it's you and me who'll have to be Prince and Princess.'

'Aren't you the lucky ones?' Anna said and

smiled, but Laura looked at her son's partner as if she were a sandwich short of a picnic.

'Anna, I'm afraid you don't have a clue what these two are fighting,' she whispered. 'Oh, my dears, I wish I could help. But Matty…yes, until Rafael and your mama work themselves out then I guess we're it.'

In the end, keeping herself to herself was easy. She just had to be ruthless. She just had to say no firmly to Matty and walk away.

The castle libraries were amazing. Distressed and confused on that first morning, while Laura took Matty down to the stables to chat to the horses and to listen to his adventures in Australia, Kelly roamed the shelves and found tomes and documents and charts that could keep a historian happy for a century or more.

She blocked out the sound of Matty's voice drifting up from the courtyard. She blocked out the sound of the men's voices unloading the trucks, Rafael giving orders, Anna arguing…

The gong sounded for lunch but she'd already warned Cook and Matty that she seldom stopped for lunch. She didn't want to be part of that big familiar kitchen again. She worked on, trying to figure where to start. Maybe cataloguing to begin with. Mindless work while she got her bearings.

At about three in the afternoon she decided the castle was silent and she might conceivably have the kitchen to herself. She went down to make herself a sandwich.

She didn't have the kitchen to herself. Rafael was seated alone at the vast table. He had a bottle of beer before him, and the remnants of a sandwich.

She blinked. Prince Regent of Alp de Ciel with a beer and a sandwich?

He looked up as she entered, like a kid who'd been caught in a crime.

'I'm sorry,' she said, suppressing an involuntary smile, and tried to back out.

'I know. I should be eating caviare patties and drinking champagne,' he said mournfully. 'But I kinda like beer. I'm happy to share, though. I'm not sure where the caviare is, but the makings of sandwiches are in the first refrigerator.'

'I don't need…'

'If you're like me, you do need. It's just the whole company bit that worries you.'

She hesitated. Okay, it would be surly to back away now. She might as well eat. 'So why does it worry you?' she asked.

'It's not as bad as it used to be,' he admitted. 'Castle meals used to be a nightmare. A dining table twenty feet long with a damned great epergne set in the middle of it, so you couldn't see who was at the far end. The minute Kass died my mother decreed that everyone—servants and all—would eat in here. Actually, until Kass died Matty would mostly eat at the dower house, but now Kass is dead my mother thinks Matty's place is here.'

'Matty thinks his place is here,' she said cautiously and he nodded.

'Yeah. How to give a man a guilty conscience...' He swigged his beer from the bottle and watched her make a sandwich.

'So where's Anna?' she asked.

'Gone.'

'Already?'

'I'm guessing she thinks she might get stuck if she stays any longer,' he said. 'She came under protest, to make sure the more delicate bits of equipment were treated with respect. She hates that I'm staying. She gave me a blast and a half and then she retreated. She wants me to go back to Manhattan to talk to the kids.'

'And will you?'

'Not until after the coronation,' he said

morosely. 'And even then…there's a vast amount to do here. Sure, I don't want to care. I think I'm forced to. I don't have an attic.'

'Don't give me a hard time,' she growled. 'And, by the way, don't try kissing me again.'

'That was a mistake,' he agreed gravely.

'It certainly was.'

He watched her, considering. 'You didn't like it just a little bit?'

'No.'

His eyes creased at the corners, with just the faintest hint of lurking laughter. 'Liar.'

'I fell in love with Kass,' she reminded him. 'One de Boutaine in a lifetime is enough.'

It took the teasing right away from his eyes. The laughter disappeared.

'You kissed me because I look like Kass?'

'Why else would I kiss you?'

'Right,' he said flatly. 'Right.'

'And you kissed me because?' She shouldn't ask, she thought, but the question had just sort of popped out before she could stop it.

'God knows,' he said bluntly. He shrugged. 'God knows why I want to kiss you again now.'

'You want to kiss me again now?' Her voice broke on a squeak.

'I do,' he conceded. 'Maybe it's because I find your sweater almost irresistibly sexy.'

She looked down at her shapeless wool smock and she winced. It really was dreadful. She'd bought it mid-winter at a clearance sale and wore it for comfort. It was almost as old as Matty. Until now, she'd never worn it out of doors.

Once it had been crimson but it had faded with constant washing so now was a dreary pink. There was a moth hole in the bottom hem. She'd worried it a bit and the hole had extended.

'Who knows what would happen if I ever saw you in lingerie,' Rafael said bluntly. 'Though, by the look of that sweater, I can only imagine what your lingerie's like.' He shook his head, set his beer bottle aside and rose. 'A man could go hot and cold just thinking about it. I think I need to go and take a cold shower. If you'll excuse me…'

'So there'll be no more kissing?' she whispered before she could stop herself and thought frantically, Why did I do that? It was as if she was pushing to extend the conversation. Which surely she wasn't.

She hadn't.

'If you're kissing me back because I look like Kass, what do you think?' he said heavily and left her to her sandwich.

It was the pattern of their days. Working on their private projects. Avoiding each other.

In a way it was the ideal method of getting to know her son, Kelly thought as the days progressed. Matty had his own life mapped out in this castle. Up until now he hadn't had a mother and hadn't really seen the need for one. To have her thrust upon him, demanding a part of his life, would be likely to overwhelm him.

But Matty loved the idea that he had a mother. He was disappointed that she didn't seem interested in his passion—which was definitely horses—but the rest... He took to including her rooms as part of his domain. He followed the routine set down before his father had died— rigid meal times, introductory school work, working with Crater—but in between he'd hurry up to his mother's rooms to report the latest news, to make her feel included.

He was a gracious, loving little boy, Kelly thought. She was blessed. And when, at the end of the first week, he announced that Marguerite had sore legs and she couldn't go very far and would Mama like to come with him instead on his afternoon walks, Kelly thought this was as good as it got.

She had her son again. She didn't have to include herself any more than occasionally in the life of the castle.

She could swallow guilt about the load Rafael was carrying. He was still a de Boutaine, and the way he made her feel scared her witless. She was right to stay aloof.

But, 'Why don't you like my Uncle Rafael?' Matty asked as he skipped ahead through the fabulous woodland around the castle and she thought, uh-oh, had it been as obvious as that?

'I don't not like him.'

'You haven't even seen his dungeon.'

'He hasn't asked me.'

'Yes, he did. He asked you to see it on the day all his tools arrived and you didn't say anything. It's really cool down there. You should see the things he's making. He's working on a new base at the moment that will fit spaceships. He says I can have the pro… prot…protype.'

'Prototype?'

'Yes,' Matty said in satisfaction. 'Will you come and see it?'

'I think your Uncle Rafael is too busy for visitors.'

'That's silly,' Matty said and tucked his hand confidingly into hers. 'I want to show you the…prototype. Can you come and see when we get back from the walk?'

There was a cost, she thought. She'd accepted Matty's invitation to walk with him with pleasure. How could she make the boundaries clear when she kept crossing them?

He was looking up at her, anxious, sensing that things weren't right. 'My Uncle Rafael is very kind,' he said, as if he felt the need to reassure her.

'I'm sure he is.'

'He might even make you something.'

'He makes things for children.'

'And for big kids too,' Matty said. 'Aunt Laura and I read about Robo-Craft on the Internet. It says it's for kids from five to a hundred and five. How old are you?'

'Twenty-nine,' she said faintly.

'See,' Matty said. 'It's perfect for you. You will come and see it, won't you? Oh, look, Mama! There's a deer with a baby.'

* * *

He was finding it really hard to concentrate. There were so many intrusions.

Back in Manhattan, the intrusions had all been work-related. They'd been annoying but Anna had protected him from the worst and they hadn't taken him out of his head like the intrusions here.

He was trying to develop a new base. He had it almost right. Manhattan was gearing up for production for the Christmas rush—that meant he had to get it perfect by the end of this month.

But so far today he'd had Matty three times, Crater twice about finances for the treasury and now an alderman from the town with a list a mile long and a need to talk to him about land stabilization above Zunderfied.

He knew nothing about land stabilization.

He had to learn.

At the end of the basement room there was a narrow window almost at ceiling level. It was ground level outside.

He could see Kelly and Matty out on the far side of the forecourt, heading into the woods.

For one daft minute he felt an almost irresistible urge to join them.

Yeah. As if he needed domesticity added to his duties.

He had to focus.

'Maybe we need to get the land surveyed,' the man said. 'There are some who say the need is urgent. What if we contact the university and see if we can get experts to tell us what they think?'

'Who says the need is urgent?' Rafael asked uneasily, still looking out of the window. They looked great, he thought—Kelly and Matty.

She was still wearing that appalling sweater.

'Only a couple of the old men,' the alderman said soothingly, but he still looked anxious. 'There seems no immediate threat. I'll contact the university.'

'Let's do that immediately,' Rafael said, thinking about the raw scar above the town and feeling more uneasy. 'Can you set that in train? If we offer generous funding we should get people here straight away.'

The man's anxious look faded. He left, relieved, and Rafael turned again to his mechanical base.

His mind wasn't on it.

Instead, he stared out of the window again. Kelly and Matty were out there somewhere.

And a little town with erosion above it and waterlogged soil.

There was nothing more he could do. Was there? Damn.

And then they came. The knock on the door was more tentative than Matty's usual bang, but that was the only unusual part. Before he could respond, Matty had the door open and was dragging his mother inside.

'He's here. You don't have to wait. He always says come in. Uncle Rafael, Mama has come to look at your prototype.'

Matty was tugging his mother by the hand. Kelly looked completely disoriented, embarrassed, confused…

Adorable.

He could so easily slip into this, he thought. He could pick up where his cousin had left off.

Right. As if Kelly would ever want that. And where did that leave him? Right in the middle of the royal mess with no way of walking, even after twenty years.

Maybe he could have a good time for twenty years.

'Hi,' he said and smiled and she looked even more confused. Even more adorable.

'Matty wanted to show me your toys.'

'Would you like a guided tour?'

She gazed round, clearly astonished. 'It's a workshop.'

It was. The big underground cavern had been transformed. Back in Manhattan, he'd had a workshop set apart from the normal production premises, specially set up so he could have time alone to think, to work peaceably on his latest ideas. He'd had the entire contents transported here. Anna had supervised the shift. Nothing had gone wrong, and already he had a work-place he loved.

And he had the work he loved. His father had introduced him to woodwork, and to rudimentary mechanics. The two of them had worked together when Rafael was a kid, in the slivers of time his father had been able to spare from his royal duties.

Those slivers of time had seemed like gold. They'd instilled in Rafael a love of working with his hands, and now it was the place he found peace.

Did Kelly find such peace in her books?

'You know how Robo-Craft works?' he asked her.

'I've seen it in the shops,' Kelly said and that was enough encouragement for Matty to gasp in shock and drag her to the table.

'You mean you don't even know how it works? Look, Mama. It's very, very wonderful. Uncle Rafael invented it all by himself.'

He set a tiny mechanism on the middle of the table, then grabbed a sizeable plank, balanced it on top of the mechanism and flipped the switch.

The plank swung round like a slow ceiling fan.

'Now look,' Matty ordered and fiddled with the controls.

The plank swayed like a drunken ceiling fan.

'And now…'

The mechanism lifted, rolled. Amazingly the plank stayed balanced. The whole thing started moving steadily to the side of the table.

'Will it go up?' Matty demanded.

'I suspect our plank is too heavy for launch,' Rafael said. 'Why not make something that looks like a rocket? Make it a bit lighter than the plank. In fact, make it a lot lighter than the plank.'

Matty was already gazing round the room, looking for materials.

'Can I use that?' he asked, pointing to some plywood.

'Go right ahead. Here's a hacksaw and here's some craft glue. Kelly, are you going to watch?'

But Kelly was gazing at the little mechanism with longing. It looked awesome.

'Can I make a bus?' she asked and he grinned at the wistfulness in her voice. He loved it when he caught a kid's attention, even if that kid was twenty-nine years old.

'Any special reason why you'd like to make a bus?'

'It's just that rolling action. I had to spend hours on a school bus when I was a kid and the thing bucketed just like your plank. I reckon I could make a bus to sit on it and…'

'Go right ahead,' he said and beamed and she was sucked in, hook, line and sinker.

What followed was peace.

It was probably the first time Rafael had felt at peace since he'd heard of Kass's death.

He'd always found solace in his work—it had always been an escape for him—but for the past few weeks he hadn't been able to disappear. Even when he was alone, when the demands of his new role weren't pounding on his door, his conscience was doing its own pounding. So was his worry for the future—for the fact that he had no choice in the role he was expected to play. He worked with his hands down here but even as he worked his thoughts wriggled and twisted and tried to find an escape.

But just here…just for now…there was no need to escape. He had no wish to escape. This was great.

Kelly and Matty were totally entranced. They had the material they needed. They sat on high stools at his biggest work bench, their heads bent over their projects, deep in concentration.

He'd hardly seen the similarity between mother and son, but he saw it now. The way their brows creased together, puckering into a tiny line just above their noses. The way they focused absolutely. When they picked up the hacksaws and made their first tentative notch, then paused and held the plywood out to make sure they were doing the right thing, their actions were identical.

They looked…

Like mother and son.

More. They looked endearing. Enchanting. He was giving them both pleasure and the thought was enough to settle a deep, aching pain in his gut that had been there…maybe ever since his father had died.

A measure of the success of Robo-Craft was that it pulled people in regardless. If you could put a plain, unadorned plank on this tiny mechanism and watch it transform into something that suggested an old school bus or a spaceship—anything—and if you could see that very easily you could make such a thing and watch it work…

'Yeah, it's brilliant,' Kelly said, smiling, and he grinned at her across the table.

'Was it that obvious?'

'That you love this stuff. Yes, it is. I can see why Anna's cross at you being dragged back here.'

'Uncle Rafael wants to be here,' Matty said stoutly. He'd glued four pieces of wood together and was now chopping a nose cone out of Styrofoam with his hacksaw. His tongue was out a little, to the side; he was concentrating fiercely, but he was ready to join in this adult conversation. 'You both want to be here, don't you?'

'Because you're here,' Kelly said warmly. 'Yes, we do.'

Easy for you to say, Rafael thought, but out of deference to Matty he didn't say it.

They returned to work. Rafael concentrated on

trying not to watch the pair of them. He had his own work to do and he was free to do it.

He'd rather watch them.

'Mama, Crater says you really can ride horses,' Matty said into the silence and the atmosphere in the workshop changed.

'I can't,' Kelly said shortly.

'He said you rode with my papa.'

'That was a long time ago. I've forgotten.'

'I could help you to remember,' Matty said, considering the shape of his cone and sandpapering a little off one side. 'Crater said he saw you the first morning you met my papa. He said Papa rode Blaze and you rode a horse called Tamsin. Crater said he saw you gallop up the mountain and he said you looked just like a prince and a princess.' He wrinkled his nose over his wobbly cone. 'How can you forget how to ride?'

'What happened to Tamsin?' Kelly asked before she could help herself.

'Papa sold her,' Matty said, disapproving. 'I asked once and he got angry and yelled at me. But there's more horses in the stables you could ride. When Papa had other ladies here they rode with him. You could ride one of their horses.'

'Matty, when I get on a horse,' Kelly said, concentrating on her plywood school bus, 'I forget to be sensible.'

'Me, too,' Matty said cheerfully. 'Papa says when I'm on a horse I'm a true prince. He says I have royal hands.' He looked down at his fingers, covered liberally with craft glue. 'What do you think he means by that?'

'You have blue blood,' Rafael said, trying to deflect attention from Kelly. She'd forgotten she was enjoying herself. She looked as if she wanted to bolt again, back to her books and her attic.

'I don't have blue blood, silly,' Matty reproved. He held up his forefinger for inspection—it had a sticking plaster over its tip. 'Yesterday, I tried to carve a nose cone with Uncle Rafael's big knife,' he told Kelly. 'There was a man in here talking to Uncle Rafael and I borrowed his knife without asking. My finger slipped and my blood was really, really red.'

'You didn't tell me,' Kelly said, startled, and thought that a real mother would have noticed.

'Uncle Rafael says it's our own secret,' he said with a guilty look at Rafael. Then, clearly anxious to change the subject, he turned to Rafael. 'Why don't you ride horses?'

'I just don't,' Rafael said flatly.

'Crater said you used to.'

'Crater says too much for his own good,' Rafael growled.

'He said you rode with your papa. But then your papa was hurt really badly on a horse. Was that when you stopped riding?'

'I stopped riding when I decided that riding royal horses was for royals,' Rafael said.

'You're royal.'

'Yes, but only a little bit royal. Not as royal as you, and I'd rather be a toy-maker.'

'You'll be a more important royal even than me until I'm twenty-five. I thought that and Crater said yes.'

'You're too clever for your own good.'

'Yes,' Matty said, satisfied with Rafael's opinion. 'So you'll be a very important prince for years and years. You could ride lots and lots in that time. We could get Mama another horse called Tamsin…'

'I don't want a horse,' Kelly managed.

'Why not?' Matty demanded, astonished. 'Papa said it's royal to ride horses. Good horses. He said it's in our blood. Real royals learn to ride before they walk.'

'But I'm not royal,' Kelly said flatly and set her

bus down so hard the unset craft glue gave up its tenuous hold and it disintegrated into four separate pieces. 'I need to go back to work.'

'You haven't finished your bus,' Rafael said gently.

'No,' she whispered. 'And I'm not going to. I shouldn't be here. Discussing royal blood. Discussing royal horses. For a moment there I almost forgot who I am. Thank you, Matty, for reminding me.'

She should destroy every gown in her old suite, she thought savagely as she made her way back to her rooms. They were too much of a temptation. She should never have put on that little black dress. But there were so many more gowns, hanging there...

Waiting.

CHAPTER SEVEN

AFTERWARDS—after a dinner where Kelly hadn't appeared, pleading lack of appetite, when his mother had returned to the dower house, when Matty was well in bed, the servants had dispersed for the night and there seemed little risk of him being disturbed—Rafael wandered down to the stables. It was almost as if a magnet were pulling him. Matty's conversation had stirred something within him that he'd thought he'd buried long since.

Riding was royal? He'd never thought of it as such. Riding was the thing he'd done with his father, an extension of his legs, a merging of himself and the wonderful animal beneath him.

Until that day…

He remembered it still in his dreams. Kass had been here with a group of his friends, and Rafael, at fifteen, had been home from boarding school. His parents had always been uneasy about him being here when Kass was home. As Rafael had been. He'd loathed his ego-driven cousin and he hadn't needed his parents' encouragement to steer clear of him.

On the last day of his holidays Rafael and his father had risen early, planning to ride up to the lower foothills where they could see the sun rise over the Alps. It was something they'd done every time Rafael left—a small personal ritual that both pretended meant little but in truth they'd both loved.

They'd set out in the pre-dawn dimness, walking their horses carefully through the woodland, speaking softly, half-awed by the early morning hush.

The shot had come from nowhere, zinging over the horses' heads, terrifying in the stillness. Later, Rafael had found the track of the bullet in the hide of his father's big gelding. The horse had been grazed across the neck. No wonder he'd reared, terrified, lunging backward, hurling his rider back with a savagery and ferocity no rider could cope with unprepared.

Rafael's father had been thrown against the trunk of an oak, an unyielding, implacable barrier. A lower branch had ripped his face. The solid trunk had crushed his spine.

Rafael had him in his arms when Kass and his cronies had burst through the undergrowth. It seemed they'd been drinking all night and had decided bed was boring—they'd do a little pre-dawn hunting before sleeping off the drink. They had been mounted on the royal horses—horse-flesh worth millions.

Each and every one of them had been carrying a loaded gun, but only Kass's had been discharged. His friends had seemed appalled, but Kass had either been too drunk or too arrogant to care. He'd stared down at Rafael and his father and he'd sneered, 'You ride in my woods, you expect what you get. Surely he should know how to hold his seat by now. That's the commoner side of the family coming out.'

He'd turned his horse and cantered off, uncaring, leaving his companions, who had more conscience than he did, to cope with an almost fatally injured man and his distraught son.

It was the last time Rafael had been on a horse. The commoner side of him had decided right there that the non-royal part of him was the only side he cared about.

'You hate them as much as I do,' a soft voice said behind him and he whirled.

'Kelly.'

'Matty said he left his sweater here,' she said. She hesitated and then walked forward to where a crimson sweater lay crumpled on the oat bin.

'The servants would have fetched it.'

'I don't do servants.' She lifted the sweater, holding it against her almost as a shield. She walked back towards the door, but then she turned.

'Your mother told me you hate the horses,' she murmured. She was standing in the doorway, a shadow against the moonlight outside. 'She told me why.'

'I don't hate them. I just…don't ride. And you?'

'I don't ride either.'

'Crater said you do.'

'Crater said I did. Past tense.'

'You know why I don't ride,' he said, as a mare behind him nuzzled his hair, pressuring him to pay her attention. 'That's a bit lopsided.'

'I used to love horses,' she whispered. 'That's what got me into trouble.'

'I don't understand.'

'I don't…'

'Tell me, Kelly,' he said urgently. There was a moment's silence while she thought about it, and then she shrugged.

'The morning after I met Kass…' she ventured, not moving from her doorway. 'That first day, he came out of the castle dressed like you were that day back at the gold-diggings. In his dress sword and medals. He looked gorgeous. He seemed angry—but then he seemed to change. He sat by me as I worked and he asked question after question, like he was fascinated. I couldn't believe he was interested in me or my work. But he was and he took me out to dinner that night and I felt so special…you wouldn't believe. He asked me to sleep with him—well, of course—but I had enough sense to hold back on that one. And then he asked me to ride at dawn.'

'I…I see.'

'Maybe you do and maybe you don't,' she said listlessly. 'I was an only kid. My parents were academics—true academics—almost reclusive. My father had inherited enough to keep us financially secure, so they spent their lives studying. We lived in a house chock-full of books, as far from civilisation as it was possible to get while allowing for emergency dashes to get more books. Our cottage was on a hundred acres, near no one. I was an accident. The only reason I made it into the world was that my mother was so preoccupied with her studies she didn't realize she was pregnant until it was too late to do anything about it. They barely tolerated me. Their only pleasure in me was the amount I could learn, and my only pleasure was horses.'

'How did that happen?'

'You can't have a farm without animals,' she said, talking flatly, as if it was a dreary little story that affected someone else—some stranger. 'Or some method of keeping the grass down. My parents wanted the solitude but not the bother. So they rented the land to a local horse stud. There were horses everywhere. I loved them. The farmer's name was Matt Fledgling and it's no accident I agreed to call my son Matty for I'll remember Matt with gratitude for ever. Anyway, when I was about eight and spending hour upon hour talking to horses that were three times as tall as me, Matt took pity on me and taught me to ride. From then on, Matt let me help exercise his stock. He said, rightly or wrongly, that I was doing him a favour. His horses were mostly gallopers, racehorses, thoroughbreds, and I loved them. So when Kass asked me to ride… Oh, I said yes, and he put me on a mare who was the most wonderful horse I'd ever ridden. We went high up into the Alps. I was showing off. I didn't care. It was my skill, and I was with a prince who was taking notice of me, who was looking at me as if he thought I was beautiful. I can't tell you what an aphrodisiac it was.

'And then it all fell in a heap,' she whispered. 'My arrogance. My pride. My delight in showing off. Look where it got me. My parents said the only true friend anyone has is a book. Boring but dependable.'

'Boring's right,' Rafael said and she cast an angry glance at him.

'It's my choice.'

'It doesn't have to keep being your choice.'

'So what would you have me do?' she demanded.

'You might try being a human,' he snapped. 'Being a mother to your son.'

'I am.'

'You're not. Bolting up to your garret whenever things get personal. Staying in the background like the good little girl your parents wanted you to become. They've succeeded, haven't they,

Kelly? You're as afraid to come out of your books as they are.'

'You won't get on a horse.'

'And you won't even make a wooden school bus. Hell, Kelly, life's not for fearing.'

'I don't fear…'

'You're terrified. Even your wardrobe full of fabulous gowns. You're terrified of them.'

'I do what I have to do to protect myself.'

'You do what you have to do to make yourself miserable. Kelly, you could be so much.'

'No.'

'It's true,' he said and, before she could react, he'd crossed the gap between them. She looked like a waif, he thought. A lost soul, out of place, wondering where on earth her place was.

'Maybe it's time you tried life,' he said as he reached forward to take her in his arms.

Third time lucky?

Third time true.

For Rafael, at least, this was a measured, certain step. He'd been watching her in the doorway, a fleeting shadow looking as if she might melt away into the night. And suddenly, as he'd watched her, the way he felt about her formed a tangible shape, a vision of what she could be if she could just set her fear aside.

Underneath the hurt and fear there was a woman, a lovely sprite of a woman, who could laugh with her son, who could dress to the nines, who could be a true royal princess and enjoy it. Who could live!

If only she could break through that armour plating she'd built so carefully around herself. A psychologist might have some hope of breaking it down—doing it the right way. Not Rafael. He had no weapons against it, other than the weapon his body was telling him he had—the fact that she was all woman and he was seeing her as she should be. The fact that she'd been Kass's woman, that she was someone he'd sworn never to touch, dissipated in that one moment of insight, and all that was left was warmth and heat and desire.

Quite simply, he wanted her as he'd wanted no other woman. The first time he'd seen her, in her appalling moleskin dungarees, in her mud and grime, he'd felt this strange link that had done nothing but grow and grow.

He reached her now, but he reached for her slowly, giving her room to back off if she would.

For even now, even wanting her as much as he did, he'd not coerce her. He'd not frighten her any more than she'd been frightened.

But she was braver than she thought she was. He knew that about her. She was a strong, determined woman and under that cold armour she was as needful as he. Maybe even needful of the same thing. To hold herself aloof for six long years—longer—all her life, if you didn't think of that one appalling encounter with his cousin…

His hands caught her waist and he held. But, instead of kissing her straight away, he simply looked down at her, holding her at arm's length in the moonlight, asking her a wordless question with his eyes.

She gazed up at him, seemingly troubled. But not pulling away. Asking her own questions— questions it seemed she couldn't answer.

'I very much want to kiss you,' he whispered and she gazed up at him in bewilderment.

'Rafael, why?'

'You're beautiful.'

'Right,' she said, self-mocking, and he looked down at her appalling sweater and smiled.

'We could take that off.'

'In your dreams.'

'You are in my dreams,' he whispered. 'Hell, Kelly, even in that damned disgusting garment you're in my dreams. Imagine where we'd be without it.'

'In diabolical trouble. Rafael, I don't want this.'

She didn't mean it. He could hear it in her voice—the uncertainty, the doubt.

'What is it about me you don't want?' he asked and waited for her to think about it. For his own doubts were dissolving.

He'd always thought of her as Kass's woman. He'd sworn he could never have anything to do with Kass, but he knew now that Kass was a tiny part of her past, a nightmare that maybe he could help vanquish. The more he knew of her, the more he saw her just as Kelly. Kelly in her disgusting dungarees, Kelly in her hoops and crinoline, Kelly in her Audrey Hepburn gown, Kelly with her tongue out to the side as she adjusted the sides of her school bus…

'I glued your bus together,' he told her. 'It works magnificently. Come and see it tomorrow.'

'I can't.'

'Why can't you?'

'I just…don't trust myself.'

'Then trust me.'

'How can I trust you?' she said with sudden asperity. 'I only came here because I thought you were a womanizing toad like all the de Boutaines are, and you'd deflect the media away from me and my son. Then you tell me you have a partner—how deceitful is that? And then she's not even your partner. She's as fed up with you as I am and deservedly so. Tell me how I can trust a man like that?'

'You can.'

'I know I can and it scares me stupid,' she said and her voice was a wail.

He smiled. He pulled her against him and held—simply held her—asking nothing, expecting nothing, just resting his chin on her hair, breathing in the scent of her, waiting for her heart to settle, for her to decide that yes, she could trust, yes, maybe she could lift her face and be kissed.

'It's too soon,' she whispered and he nodded gravely.

'Of course it's too soon.'

'I don't even know you.'

'You married Kass within…'

'See, even you,' she spat and hauled herself away from his grip and glared. He had, it seemed, made a bad tactical error. 'I married

Kass fast. I was a fool. You think I'll jump into bed with you…'

'I haven't even asked…'

'You don't have to ask. You want. Don't you?'

'Yes,' he agreed gravely for he could do nothing else. He definitely wanted.

'And just because you're here you expect me to kiss you.'

'I'm just sort of hoping.'

'Well, stop hoping.'

'I can't,' he said honestly. 'Kelly, I can't. Like you, I thought this was crazy. I never thought I'd feel like this about you, but I do.'

'You're just doing it to suck me in.'

'Why would I do that?'

'Because you want someone to share the limelight. Share the throne.'

'You told me I had to pick gorgeous young women. Models and such. Not someone—' he hesitated, aware it behoved him to act cautiously '—in a really, really big sweater.'

She gave a gasp that ended on choked laughter, quickly suppressed. 'I won't share royalty. I won't share the limelight.'

'If you keep wearing that sweater you should be fine,' he reassured her, but her glare intensified.

'If I'm anywhere near you…'

'They'll take photographs of my sword. Not of you.'

'Rafael, I don't want it!'

'You don't want what, my love?'

'You,' she wailed. 'I don't trust myself. You stand there and you look so gorgeous and you smile at me, and I shouldn't have come to the stables—I shouldn't—but I saw you come and it was like I was just pulled. Matty's sweater was just an excuse. See? How stupid is that? And I know I just have to move an inch and you'll kiss me senseless.'

'Less than an inch.'

'And it's taken me years to get away from it,' she continued, refusing to be deflected. 'How can I re-establish a relationship with Matty when the whole royal goldfish bowl is operating around us? How can I make sense of what's happened?'

'Maybe we could kiss in private?' he said, without much hope and she glowered.

'Right. Any minute you'll ask me to get back on a horse.'

'You want to.'

'As you do,' she snapped.

'I don't.'

'Then it's for very sensible reasons. Like mine. Rafael, we're all wrong for each other.'

'We feel right.'

'I'm going to bed,' she snapped. The mare behind them gave a sharp whinny. She glanced past him at the horse and her expression softened.

'You still love them,' he said gently.

'Because I'm pathetic,' she admitted. 'I keep thinking of Tamsin.'

'Not of Kass?' he said, suddenly hopeful, and she shook her head.

'Not of Kass. Never of Kass. I think all this trouble started with a horse. I need my head read to be here now, with you. With the horses.'

'And yet you're here.'

'I…'

'Kelly,' he said and he placed his hands on either side of her face; he stooped and kissed her gently on the mouth. It was over before she could object, a feather kiss of reassurance, nothing more. Demanding nothing. Expecting nothing.

But the beginning of loving.

'Kelly, work it out,' he said softly. 'Take your time. I'll not rush you. For me…I think I'm falling in love. I didn't intend to. In fact, it's the last thing I intended. But hey, it's happening. I know what's before us is hard. But maybe… maybe we could do it together. Maybe we could even give this royalty thing a go. Given time. Given trust.'

'Yeah? Like riding again,' Kelly said and she knew she sounded bitter but she couldn't help it. 'How many years will it take before you get on a horse?'

'We don't have to ride before we trust each other.'

'We don't have to do anything,' Kelly said and then, with a tiny sound between a laugh and a sob, she tugged away. 'Please, Rafael, don't do this. I'm not royal. I never, ever should have learned to ride. I never, ever should have met Kass. And I never, ever should give my heart to anyone but my son. That's all I want. I'm not royal. I'm not part of this household. I'm just me.'

And, before he could say a word in response, she turned and fled.

He let her go. There was nothing else to do. For he even agreed with her.

He didn't want to be royal. How could he persuade Kelly to be something he didn't want himself?

He couldn't.

But things had changed. Or maybe they hadn't

changed but he'd suddenly seen them for what they really were.

He'd suddenly seen inside his heart, and what he saw there… It was terrifying, but then again, he wouldn't want it any other way.

Kelly…

Kelly. Princess Kellyn Marie de Boutaine.

Could he persuade her to take on the royal role a second time? He must.

But how?

The Prince Regent of Alp de Ciel stood in the doorway of the stables, looking across the empty palace forecourt for a very long time.

CHAPTER EIGHT

WHERE there was a death and a new Crown Prince, there was also a coronation. Rafael had put it off for as long as possible but it had to be faced. In the days that followed, as Kelly retreated to her study, as the routine of the palace formed some semblance of normality, Crater's insistence that the coronation take place had to be considered.

'Matty's far too young,' Rafael growled when it was first brought up.

'You'll be at his side,' Crater told him. 'You make the vows on his behalf. It will be you who carries them out until he's twenty-five.'

'And what about his mother?'

'Kellyn wishes to be treated as a commoner,' Crater said. 'She'll attend but not in an official capacity.'

'She's still officially Kass's widow. She should have a place in the ceremony.'

'See if you can persuade her,' Crater said. 'I can't.'

And neither could Rafael. In truth, since the night in the stables he hardly saw her. Matty spent time with her, but she'd intensified her planned routine of study and self-containment.

She'd opened herself a little, he thought. In doing so she'd terrified herself and had then retreated.

He hated it. He hated that she hid herself away. Damn her parents, he thought, and wondered if it wasn't too late to find them and horsewhip them. Damn Kass for being dead so he couldn't do the same to him.

He felt like weeping on her behalf—for the stupid waste of it, for the fact that the laughing, happy woman she could be had been repressed in such a brutal manner.

And damn if the weather didn't agree with him. The glorious sunshine that had greeted their arrival had given way to steady dripping rain, making everything grey, dreary and waterlogged.

Not the best time for a coronation.

'There'll never be a perfect time,' Crater told him. 'But I've approached each of the royal houses of Alp d'Azuri, Alp d'Estella and Alp de

Montez. The royals are all available at the end of this month. If we leave it much longer, Phillippa, the Princess Royal of Alp d'Estella, risks being confined with their first child. Max won't leave her. We need their presence.'

'Why?'

'If we're to gain any economic strength,' Crater said tentatively, 'we need to get the four countries working together. It was a dream of your father's. Until now I've hardly dared to hope the four Alp countries could become a Federation. But if you brought in reforms to bring Alp de Ciel into line with them politically…'

'Hey…'

'It would take commitment on your part,' Crater said. 'But you've come this far.'

'I don't want…'

'To commit yourself yet,' Crater said hurriedly, clearly not wanting him to veto a dream in an instant. 'But if we have the coronation soon and we have Raoul and Max and Nikolai and Rose here… It seems a wonderful opportunity.'

'You're steamrollering me.'

'No, sir,' Crater said sadly, 'I can't. I'm just saying it's a dream you might wish to pursue. Meanwhile, this coronation has to happen. The country's expecting it. Can I announce that it'll be on the twenty-sixth of this month?'

'Fine,' Rafael growled. 'But there's no way I can sit up in the back in the dark like someone else we could mention?'

'No, sir,' Crater said firmly. 'No chance at all.'

'Come and see.'

Kelly was mid-manuscript. The pages dated from the seventeenth century. They should be locked away in a temperature-controlled vault. Instead, they'd been sitting in the bookshelves here for the last four hundred years, an unnoticed, untouched treasure trove.

It was historian heaven. She should be in heaven.

Instead, she was lonely and bored. If she could pick Matty up and take him back to the goldfields it'd be great, she thought. Other than that, she had to bury herself in the studies her parents had loved, but every time there were voices in the forecourt she'd look down and sometimes it'd be Rafael and she thought her equilibrium had been messed with for ever.

Somehow she had to restore it. She had to forget those dangerous kisses and get on with…her boring life.

But here was Matty, at a time when he was scheduled for a lesson with Crater, bursting into her room and grabbing her hand and tugging her after him.

'Mama, the clothes are here. For the coronation. They're here, they're here, and Ellen says I have to try them on now, and there's a sword just like my Uncle Rafael's. It's splendid. Mama, you have to see.'

Bemused, she let him lead her downstairs, along the corridor to the workrooms behind the kitchen. She could hear the murmur of women's voices as she approached, and she relaxed. Matty's coronation outfit had been a source of interest and enthusiasm for the last week. Needlewomen had come in from Zunderfied and the castle had been humming.

'You should have something royal to wear,' Crater had said, reproving, but there was no way she was going down that road. She'd married in simple clothes in Paris. She'd never been a royal bride.

She wasn't royal now.

Matty was tugging her forward, hurrying her on. He reached the big oak doors of the workrooms and threw them open.

Rafael was there.

She stopped breathing.

He was gorgeous. Stunning. Breathtakingly amazing.

A real prince.

His clothes fitted like a second skin. Deep black leggings—skintight. Glossy Hessian boots, jet-black with tassels. What looked to be a morning jacket, but inset with red, black and gold panels, intricately embroidered. The royal crest was emblazoned on the jacket breast. A deep gold sash lay across his breast. There were rows of medallions, epaulettes, gold tassels...

A sword lay at his side, longer than the one she'd seen in Australia, its grip a cunningly wrought gold three-dimensional symbol of the royal house of de Boutaine.

His black curls were flicked back as they always were, raked back by fingers that worried. He'd been gazing in the mirror, his cool grey eyes smiling, half mocking. As the door opened and he turned to see who entered, his smile still lingered.

He was laughing at himself, she thought, but there was no way she was laughing.

Rafael...

It was as much as she could do not to sink

into a curtsey. As it was, she gripped the door handle and held.

'It's a bit much,' he said, smiling across at her, and she thought wildly, Don't do that—don't smile, don't!

'Mine's just like it,' Matty said with deep satisfaction. 'Aren't we gorgeous?'

'Gorgeous,' she agreed faintly.

'What will you be wearing, Mama?' Matty asked. He crossed to where Ellen was waiting to help him into his costume. 'It'll have to be something very beautiful to match my Uncle Rafael and me.'

'I couldn't come near matching you,' she whispered.

'But you will wear a pretty dress.'

'Maybe,' she said. Thinking of those gowns. Thinking of what had happened the one night she'd worn one.

'One of the pretty ones you wore on the goldfields?' Matty said hopefully. He was in leggings now, turning to the mirror and sticking his small chest out with manly pride. 'Are they pretty enough for the coronation, Uncle Rafael?'

'No,' Rafael said.

'Then it's just as well I didn't bring them,' she retorted.

'If you please, ma'am...'

There were four women in the room. One had been adjusting the base of Rafael's coat. Two were sitting at the table sewing, and Ellen was helping Matty on with his vest. But now she interjected. She rose stiffly to her feet and stood, unsure. 'I...we have a suggestion.'

'A suggestion?' Kelly frowned and glanced suspiciously at Rafael, but he was looking as in the dark as she was.

'The clothes Prince Rafael and Prince Mathieu will wear are traditional. We wondered...seeing you're a historian...' Ellen gave a nervous gasp, looked to her friends for support and crossed to the corner of the room. There was a mannequin there, shrouded with dust-sheets.

Ellen cast Kelly another nervous glance and then she tugged off the dust-sheet.

The dress was breathtaking. It looked almost Elizabethan, a creation of the most exquisitely cut gold and ivory silk, skilfully set over a rich crimson underskirt. The neckline was almost square, cut low to reveal the swell of breasts. Filigree sleeves were gathered into elegant lace wristbands in the finest of gold. The waist cinched into a deep V, designed to make any woman's waist look tiny.

And the embroidery. Such embroidery—all fire, swirls and curves. The gown shimmered and glistened as Ellen pulled the dust-sheet free, almost assuming a life of its own. There were hoops underneath, spreading the dress almost as wide at the hem as the gown was high. There was a train—Ellen was setting it out now. It was embroidered to represent a golden dragon, running from waist to maybe ten metres behind.

Kelly gasped with shock. She couldn't help herself. She stepped forward, almost reverently, hardly brave enough to touch it.

'It's…'

'Over two hundred years old,' Ellen breathed. 'When the old Prince was pressuring Kass to be married, he ordered it to be restored. But then… then Kass married you.'

'Not a princess,' she whispered.

'But you are a princess,' Ellen said stubbornly. 'You should have had the right to wear it. You have the right to wear it now. We've measured it against your gowns here. It'll take very little alteration.'

'Wow,' Rafael breathed. 'Kelly, you have to wear it.'

'I don't,' she said, feeling so out of her depth she was close to tears. 'I'm not royal.'

'No, but you are,' Matty repeated. 'You were married to my father. You're a real princess.'

'I'm a commoner.'

'You're Australian,' Ellen said with satisfaction.

'So what?' She was bewildered. Maybe she even sounded angry, but she couldn't help it. The sight of the dress was so awesome it took her breath away. And the way Rafael was looking at her didn't help. Plus the way Rafael looked…She had a sudden vision of the two of them. Rafael in his dress uniform and she in this dress.

No and no and no.

But Ellen was speaking. She had to listen. What did being an Australian have to do with anything?

'The palace gossip was that was why Kass chose you,' Ellen said, answering her question before she'd framed it. 'When Kass's father heard of Prince Raoul's marriage to Jessica in Alp d'Azuri to a commoner—to an Australian—he laughed about it. He said Raoul was a fool and the country would never accept such a marriage. And then you and your team were working so close to here…'

'So he just picked me,' Kelly whispered.

'And we were so excited,' Ellen said stoutly. 'The people of Alp d'Azuri have had nothing but prosperity since their prince's marriage. We had such hopes…'

'Of me?'

'You were our princess from the time Prince Kass married you,' Ellen retorted. 'We hated that you went away. We've always wanted you to come home. And we hated that the old Prince made us put this gown away.' She faltered and bent her head over the train, pretending to straighten a crease. 'We…we need a royal family.'

'You have Rafael and Matty,' Kelly whispered.

'It's not a family.'

'Leave her,' Rafael said, sounding suddenly angry. 'Ellen, this isn't fair.'

'No, sir.'

'You don't need to defend me,' Kelly told him.

'Don't I?'

'No,' she flashed, and he grinned that heart-stopping grin and lifted his sword from its scabbard.

'I guess it's not me alone. You have two men to do it now,' he said, seemingly determined to turn what had been too serious a moment into a joke. 'The decision about the dress can be made later. Matty, we need you to have some fencing lessons. *En garde, petit…*'

'Not here,' Ellen shrieked as Matty picked up his sword and giggled. 'Not near the dress.'

But Rafael was changing the subject away from the dress, away from her, distracting them all from a topic she found too hard. She could merge into the background, she thought thankfully.

He was protecting her.

But…but…

We had such hopes.

She'd never thought of it from the people's point of view. She'd always believed they'd thought her a tramp. Someone they were lucky to be rid of.

She swallowed. Ellen had caught Matty's sword which, mercifully, had a blunt end. She'd put it firmly aside. Now she was manoeuvring him into a jacket that matched Rafael's.

Her two royal princes.

A family?

No. No, they weren't. Matty was her family, but he also belonged to another.

She was on the outside of that other, not even wanting to look in.

The dress was there. A dare. A challenge.

A role that was already hers.

'Come on in, the water's fine,' Rafael said softly and she blinked at him in astonishment.

'I don't…'

'I know.'

'I can't.'

'You can.'

'Rafael…'

And then the earth moved.

It was a mere tremor—a shift that made the light above Ellen's head sway slightly on its long lead from the high ceiling. A vase sitting on the edge of the mantelpiece slipped sideways and crashed on to the hearth. It left Kelly feeling just slightly off balance, as if she'd stood up too fast and felt a little dizzy, but then balance was restored and things were okay.

But the light was still swinging, casting weird shadows over the half dressed Matty. Ellen was staring upward, mesmerized by the swinging light, but Kelly was over the far side of the room in an instant, grabbing Matty to her, holding him close.

The light was still swaying. The vase was still smashed on the hearth.

'Outside,' Rafael said harshly into the stunned silence. 'Get outside, everyone—into the forecourt and away from the building.'

He didn't have to say it twice. Kelly was already moving, carrying Matty as she ran. Rafael moved to intercept her but she shook her head and kept running.

'We're fine. Get everyone out.'

She'd experienced this before—an earth tremor. It had been a small quake, measuring three on the Richter scale, and it had shaken some of her parents' beloved books from the shelves. That had been all the damage.

That was all this would be, she told herself as she ran.

'Mama…' Matty quavered.

'It's just an earth tremor,' she said, not pausing. She could put him down but he was in bare feet and she had him in her arms and that was where it felt like he belonged. She was running down the vast stone steps that led out to the forecourt. Behind her, she could hear Rafael shouting orders.

'Assemble outside, everyone, and I mean everyone. Ellen, take a roll call. Crater, go over to the dower house and see if my mother's okay.

Get her outside too. Marsha, the dogs are already outside, you go back inside and I'll come after you with a whip…'

It was just an earth tremor. A minor one. Kelly sank to the ground on the lawns beside the fore-court and looked up at the towering castle walls. This castle had stood intact for centuries. It was clearly intending to stay intact for longer. There was no movement.

'We wait outside,' Rafael commanded into the morning stillness. 'We wait.'

So they waited. Fifteen minutes. Twenty. Luckily, the constant rain of the past few days had given way to warm sunshine so waiting wasn't a hardship. Rafael had them all gathered together. He was still dressed in his royal finery.

Laura ducked back into the dower house—against her son's orders—and fetched shoes for Matty. He accepted them with gratitude, left the safety of his mother's arms—he'd clung really close while the tremors had been happening—and started to be a little prince again.

'We've had an earthquake,' he said impor-tantly. 'An earthquake's very dangerous.'

'An earth tremor,' Kelly corrected. 'Not so bad.'

'What's the difference between an earthquake and an earth tremor?'

'A tremor happens a lot,' Kelly said. 'When a little bit of the earth moves way, way down deep and everything on the top settles a bit. In an earthquake a whole lot of the earth settles. Your Uncle Rafael says we should stay outside until we're sure it won't get any worse but I think it's okay.'

Everyone else obviously did too. After half an hour standing in the sun Rafael decided it seemed safe to return to normal.

'The phone lines are down.' Crater was fretting. 'There must be damage somewhere.'

'I'll have someone check in the village,' Rafael said, but as he did there was a shout from outside the castle gates.

There was a boy running. Shouting. Rafael stepped forward to meet him.

Rafael looked like a man in charge, Kelly thought, in his full royal regalia, his dress sword still in its scabbard, his whole bearing royal. The boy ran naturally to him. He was a teenager, sixteen maybe, wide-eyed with shock and breathless with worry.

'Sir,' he gasped in his own language. 'Sir, we're in trouble. The landslip… There's been a huge landslip above the village. The houses… There are people buried. The road's blocked. Sir, you have to come. Please.'

Rafael gripped the boy's shoulder while he told his story. The boy looked to Rafael to take charge but Rafael's wonderful uniform didn't give him the local knowledge he needed now.

He'd hardly been home since he was fifteen. Crater knew the land, the people, the emergency drills. He was in his seventies but he stepped forward now and started giving orders.

The road was cut. They needed to get an assessment of what the damage was. He'd send a team to climb high above the castle to where a man could see right across the valley.

'I'll go,' Rafael said. 'I have radio gear in the workshop. I can use that to contact the outside world if the telephones stay cut. Crater, I'll give you a handset as well so I can get back to you.'

'You won't get up there.'

'I'll take a horse,' Rafael said and Kelly gasped. For him to ride again…

'The villagers might need you,' Crater said, not hearing the implications of what Rafael had said, thinking only of what was before them.

'I'll get back down and help dig, whatever you want, as soon as I can.'

'You're our prince,' Crater said obliquely. 'We'll want you in the village.'

'I'll be there as soon as I can,' Rafael said. 'Kelly, love, make sure things stay safe here. Any more tremors, you're in charge.'

She was in charge but there was nothing to do. Everyone else left. Even Laura disappeared, donning stout walking boots and going with Ellen and Marguerite down to the little village hospital to see if they could be of help.

Kelly stayed with Matty.

'We should be down in the village too,' Matty said, more and more insistently as the afternoon wore on.

'We'd just get in the way,' she told him. 'Crater's taken everyone who can dig with him. Your Uncle Rafael will be down there by now. We need to look after the castle.'

'It's cowardly to stay in the castle when our people need us.'

It did feel wrong. But every able-bodied man and woman had joined the team to go to the village, so Kelly needed to stay here with her son. Even though it killed her not to know what was happening. Where Rafael was. What had happened in the village.

'I'm the Prince and you're the Princess,' Matty told her, deeply disapproving of her decision to stay where they were. 'Crater says it's the job of a prince to lead his people.'

'You're five years old and I'm not a princess,' she said helplessly. 'Maybe we could play Scrabble.'

He looked at her calmly, figuring out whether she meant it or not and intelligent enough to see that she did.

'Okay,' he said at last. 'Will we play in your room?'

'I...yes.' Retire to her attic. 'Why not?'

'The Scrabble set's in the nursery,' he told her. 'I'll fetch it.'

Only he didn't. Kelly checked on the dogs in the kitchen—the dog Marsha had been worried about was a bitch about to whelp and Kelly had promised to check on her every half hour. The bitch was lying peaceably in her basket, with three pups already at teat.

'See, you have your priorities right,' Kelly said, bending to fondle the big dog's ears. 'Home and hearth. It'd be good if we could be of help down in the village but a mother's place is with her kids.'

The dog gave her a long lick, which cheered Kelly immeasurably. She walked up the stairs to her attic, but when she reached it Matty wasn't there yet.

She wanted to tell him about the pups.

Maybe he'd had trouble finding the Scrabble set, she thought. She walked downstairs, along to the nursery.

She was worried, and not just about Matty. She hadn't heard anything about what was happening out in the village. No one had come back. Rafael was out there somewhere in his magnificent uniform doing heroic stuff. Laura and Crater were down in the village helping. She was stuck here minding Matty.

Only where was Matty?

He wasn't in the nursery.

Suddenly she felt sick.

'Matty?' she yelled, but her voice echoed ominously around the empty halls.

'Matty…'

A clatter of horse hooves on the cobbles below drew her to the window.

'Matty!'

If he heard her scream he didn't acknowledge it. He was on a horse. Somehow he'd managed to saddle one of the smaller mares. He was firm in the saddle, his hands keeping good control, turning the mare's head towards the gate and digging his small heels into her flanks.

'Matty,' she screamed again but he was gone.

Out of the gate towards the village.

For a long moment she simply stared at the gate as if she couldn't believe what she'd seen. But she'd seen all right. Through the open window she could hear the faint clip-clop of the mare's hooves as she disappeared from sight.

Matty was gone. Into a situation of which she knew nothing.

Her son.

Since Kass had kicked her out, Kelly had had her escape in a century past, a time warp that had held her close, protecting her from outside forces. Here she'd done her best to create a sanctuary again, where the outside world belonged to those who wanted it.

She didn't want the outside world. But her son was riding into it, with the heart of a prince.

Something played back in her mind, some

crazy lesson he'd repeated to her when she'd said it didn't make much difference that he was a prince. When she'd talked to him of the possibility of staying in Australia.

'They're my people. I should be with them,' he'd said sternly. 'Crater says when there's peril that's when the people need their prince. He said in World War Two the English King and his Queen and their two little princesses should have gone to America to be safe. Only they didn't. They stayed, and every time there was bombing the King would be there, just to say to everyone be brave.'

He was right. King George's commitment to his people had possibly been the difference between submission or victory.

But Matty was too young to make such a call. He was her son. He was five years old.

He was her prince.

And so was Rafael. Somewhere out there was Rafael. With…his people? While she stayed here like some Cinderella, hiding in her attic. Being no one.

Not even brave enough to put on a dress.

All these thoughts took no more than seconds—seconds while her frightened mind came to terms with what had happened and what now must happen.

She wheeled away, taking the stairs at a run, across the forecourt to the stables. Tamsin would no longer be here but other horses would. The road would be impassable for cars. She had to ride.

She might be a nuisance in the village. She couldn't see how her presence and Matty's presence could make a difference. Her reasons for staying separate from the royal household might still hold true.

But Matty...Prince Mathieu...and Prince Rafael, Crown Prince and Prince Regent of Alp de Ciel, had decided otherwise.

What was their royal princess to do but support them?

She hit mud at the first bend after the castle and her mare reacted with alarm, seeing the damage before she did. She'd been looking ahead, not at the road, and the horse edged sideways, rearing in fright.

She looked to where the horse was looking and looked again.

There was seeping, oozing mud in the woodlands on the higher side of the road. The road was still clear but it looked as if a flood of mud-laden water had slopped down the mountainside.

The horse—a mare whose name above her stable door decreed she was Gigi—must have come this way often. She knew it was different now. She whinnied in nervousness as Kelly settled her and forced her to keep on.

They slowed. Matty was somewhere ahead but the road now had patches of silt, with small stones and bigger rocks in their path.

How fast would Matty have come? Where would he go?

And where was Rafael?

There was no other road than this. She had to follow it.

Where was everyone?

'Come on, Gigi. Come on, girl. You can do it.'

The horse flattened her ears, but responded to her reassurance and picked her way on.

And then they were at the outskirts of the village and fear was starting to wash over in waves that made her tremble. She was franti-cally trying to suppress it. Horses sense fear and she had to keep Gigi calm. But… But…

The road ran through the foothills of the moun-tains. Above and beyond, she could see rough, jagged and newly formed scarring, a mass of ripped earth as if a great chunk of the hillside had slipped from its moorings.

There was silence as they approached the township. The mare was whinnying in fear and it took all Kelly's skill to keep her from turning home.

She couldn't go home. Somewhere ahead was Matty. He'd be moving faster than she was. He wouldn't have an adult's fear that the horse might slip on loose rocks; that he might be thrown.

He was heading for the village. Heading to his people. Was Rafael before him?

And then she rounded the final curve in the hills before the village, and as she did she drew in her breath in horror.

The full extent of the slip could now be seen. It was a great gash on the hillside, starting as a thin wedge maybe a mile above, reaching down to a slash of tossed earth maybe half a mile wide. It was as if a great chunk of the earth had simply slid out from where it should have been and lurched its way towards the village.

The village… Dear God, the village.

She could see massive destruction. Huge trees uprooted, cast aside by the power of the earth.

Houses…

What had been houses.

She put her hand to her mouth, feeling ill. She wanted to stop. She wanted to block it out.

She forced herself to look.

There were people. From here they were in the distance, like ants over an anthill, looking insignificant, moving aimlessly, or simply standing on the great mounds of tumbled earth.

She saw a red coat—a sliver of crimson on a horse…

Matty.

Sick at heart, she motioned her mare forward. 'It's okay, Gigi. It's okay.'

Only of course it wasn't. She could see from here…

Houses crushed. Roads impassable…

She pressed on. The ants became people, tearing at their houses, working furiously. The mud was everywhere. They didn't notice her as she passed—tragedy was everywhere.

Matty…

She reached him. He hadn't seen her approach. He'd stopped in the middle of the road. He was still on his horse, staring before him, his eyes wide with terror.

There was another horse beside his. He was holding the reins in his hand. He looked crazily small so near such a great creature.

The horse was Blaze. Kass's stallion.

How had Blaze reached here?

Rafael?

'Matty,' she whispered and the child turned to her, his face devoid of all colour. She had him, reaching across to take him from his horse, hauling him into her arms whether he willed it or not. He came but he was still enough of a horseman—enough of a prince—to keep the reins of both the other horses in his hand.

Before them were people, men and women, attacking a vast mound of debris with their hands. The silence was broken by sobbing.

A sign on a flattened gate told her what horror they were facing.

A school. Crushed.

'Matty,' she whispered into his hair and he crumpled against her, his face soaked with tears.

'My Uncle Rafael,' he whispered against her breast. 'He's gone in there. He's gone in there and the stuff moved on top of him and no one can get him out.'

CHAPTER NINE

KELLY had spent the last five years on the gold-fields. She'd panned for gold and she'd dug. Sure she'd been a research historian, she'd spent hours at her desk, but she could handle a spade with the best of the men.

She also knew the basics of mining. She'd researched every shaft dug back at the theme park and they were authentic. She knew what the miners had done to make themselves safe a hundred and fifty years ago, and she knew what they'd had to do to make the tourist mines even safer now.

She handed Matty to the care of the women. She took a deep, steadying breath, looked at the heap of sludge they were facing and decided they risked more people being buried alive the way they were going.

The school house was built against a cliff face. The sludge had washed down the mountain from the other direction. In most places it had swept over and onward, but here the cliff face had stopped it, so it had mounded up in a vast heap, completely obscuring the school buildings.

It was one vast, unstable mass. To dig in without shoring it up as they went was the way of disaster. She rolled up her sleeves and started issuing orders.

Amazingly, the men listened. Amazingly, they did what she said.

Matty couldn't dig but he wouldn't shift from where he was. The older people in the town would have taken him into one of the undamaged homes but Matty refused. He stayed, taking care of the horses. Wanting desperately to dig himself if only his elders would let him.

The damage in the town was awful, Kelly learned as she worked, but not as catastrophic as she'd first thought. Yes, houses were crushed, but the landslip had started high up. The tremors had been felt before it had hit, and most people had been outside. The mass had moved slowly, giving people time to run to higher ground.

Two elderly couples had been killed instantly when their houses had crashed around them. There were injuries—people had been hit by the sliding mud—but the worst of the rush of earth had been over before it had hit the town.

But the school… It was on the outskirts, which meant it had been one of the first buildings to be hit. To have the children run to higher ground would have been impossible.

'There's a basement underneath,' Kelly was told by the grim-faced mayor. 'We're thinking the teacher panicked and had everyone head for the basement. Then the mud hit the front, blocking the exit. When we got here, we could hear screaming. Prince Rafael…he took a torch in. He could just make it in through a gap in the debris and we thought we could get everyone out that way. Only then the whole lot shifted and the roof came down. And now…'

'You can't hear?'

'Muffled stuff when everything's still,' the mayor told her. 'We're hoping against hope they're all down there. Twenty kids and their teacher and our Prince. And all we can do is dig.'

'Is help coming?' she asked, trying not to sound terrified.

'The roads are all blocked,' the mayor told her. 'The tremors have been felt all the way to the border so outside help isn't going to happen. We can't get equipment in.'

So they dug. It sounded simple. Moving a

small mountain of mud from over a basement. Trying not to do any more damage. Working from the outside in, so no more weight would go on to the basement roof—if indeed it had held.

There were people alive in there. When the mayor held up his hand for silence they could hear faint cries but the mass of mud stifled everything.

'If Rafael's down there…he has a radio,' Kelly said as she dug and the men around her looked at each other and didn't respond.

If he had a radio then he'd be able to communicate. He wasn't communicating. He wasn't… he couldn't be…

She dug.

It was mind-numbing work, with nothing to alleviate the fact that tons of mud had to be shifted by hand. No one thought of bringing in machinery—to cause vibrations on top of the basement would be crazy. Care was taken to distribute diggers so no further pressure was on the mass, making the risk of further falls as small as possible.

Fatalities elsewhere had been accounted for— the injured were being cared for. This was the only area where people had yet to be found.

There were twenty children missing, one schoolteacher—and Rafael.

The workers who'd been here when Rafael had gone in were grim-faced. They'd cleared an area around the stairway into the basement. What they thought had happened was that the front of the building had collapsed. The rear of the building was set hard against the cliff face, leaving no form of exit. So the children must have fled for safety downstairs.

They'd heard them calling clearly when they'd first arrived. They were safe, they were okay. So they'd hauled the mass of timber blocking the path away. As it had cleared, the teacher below had wanted to send children up, but Rafael had stopped them.

'Let me try it first,' he'd growled. 'I don't want a child halfway up if that mass above decides it's unstable.'

Which was pretty much what had happened. Armed with a torch, Rafael had disappeared into the gloom. And then another tremor had struck and the entire building and some of the cliff face behind had subsided, leaving a mountain of debris with no one knew what underneath.

Had Rafael reached the safety of the basement? Was the basement still safe? They could hear muffled cries through the rubble but it was too thick to decipher words.

Please…

Please.

Kelly dug as she'd never dug in her life before. But all around…

People were deferring to her.

'What should we do?'

'Should we send for bulldozers?'

'It doesn't seem safe but if you think we should…'

It didn't seem safe and no, she didn't think they should but that they deferred to her was astonishing. She was a historian.

A historian who knew about mine management, she conceded, but they didn't know that. She found herself snapping orders—sending people to find shoring timbers, assessing load strengths, standing back from digging every few moments to see the whole picture…

She did know what to do. The history of gold-mining was littered with tragedy and she knew enough now to prevent mindless tunnelling from parents desperate to reach their children at any cost.

But it wasn't her role as historian that these

people were reaching out to, though, she thought as she dug. It was her role as royal.

Like Matty, standing white-faced and grim just out of reach of the diggings. Every other small child had been hauled away, well out of danger. Matty had a right to be here.

Matty's duty was to be here. He knew it. It'd been instilled from birth by those around him. Today he'd acted with a gut instinct that seemed almost inbred.

'My people need me.'

Royalty might be anachronistic, totally outdated, unfair. But right now it was what these people needed.

She dug on, and the picture came to her again of the young King during the Second World War, touring the diggings. Winston Churchill with his cigar, standing on a heap of bomb site rubble with King George beside him. The King and the Prime Minister, with the people they represented.

If she left now…if she took Matty, as was her right, and left this place, left the digging to others…

It could be done. She could give orders as to how to shore up the tunnel they were working on. She could take Matty home, cuddle him until the colour came back into his face, maybe play with Rafael's toys until he forgot…

She could never do such a thing. Because Rafael was under there? Because Rafael had kissed her?

Yes, but more than that.

Because there were twenty children and their teacher trapped?

Yes, but more than that too.

Matty was right. What he had was an age-old heritage—the leadership of his people. And, by marrying Kass, she'd inherited it as well.

Sure, she could walk away. Royals had done that since time immemorial—had walked away from their royal duties, had elected to live a normal life.

But… But…

But the good ones stayed.

'The sounds are getting clearer,' someone yelled. 'There's more'n one alive.'

'That's great. So slow down,' she yelled. 'And let's increase the rate of supports. No unnecessary risks.'

'No, ma'am.'

The good ones stayed. Queen Elizabeth, taking on the throne as a young mother, a young bride. Overseeing change in the monarchy so the people had a say in the government, so monarchy wasn't an absolute.

Doing what she saw as her duty, no matter what. And in times of crisis…

Giving a focus. A sense of leadership. A sense of continuity, regardless of personal grief.

Kelly's hands had blisters on blisters. She could stop. Men were taking turns. But the fact that she was beside them was driving them forward with renewed energy. She didn't understand it, but the fact was that monarchies had endured for century after century and here she was, a princess…fighting for her two princes. One behind her, staring at his mother as if he'd like to be part of her. He'd be digging in a heartbeat, she knew, if she let him. Matty. Mathieu. Her own little prince.

And below ground…

Rafael.

They weren't digging indiscriminately. As every layer was worked through they probed cautiously before they dug, just in case…just in case…

In case Rafael hadn't made it. In case he was trapped before the entrance to the basement. In case his body was caught up in this mass of mud and sludge and mess.

The thought had her choking and fiercely hauling her arm across eyes that welled with tears before she could stop them. She paused, fighting for breath.

'Are you okay, Your Highness?' a man asked beside her and she turned and saw his eyes were red and swollen.

'You have a child down there?' she whispered.

'Two,' he muttered. 'Heidi. She's eight. And Sophie, who's six.'

'Then we have no time for tears,' Kelly managed and wiped her face again, this time with a savage determination she knew would stay with her to the end. 'We only have time to dig.'

And in the end…

In the end it happened so fast she could scarcely believe it. One minute they were digging, the next they'd reached what seemed a vast, solid door. Six feet across, eight feet long. Mounded with debris.

They'd dug across and down, but not tunnelling. They were open cut mining, completely removing the mass of dirt above and shoring the sides. It made things slower but surely safer. To tunnel in these unstable conditions would be madness, Kelly had decreed, and the red-eyed men and women around her had agreed.

So now they had a trench thirty feet long, starting at the edge of the mass of debris and working in, dropping fast, so the sides were twelve, fourteen feet high. The trench was big enough for two men to work side by side, while those behind cleared and passed the rubble back.

And now…The last few spadefuls had exposed the slab. The men in front edged shovels sideways, exploring.

Hitting wood.

'It's holding the whole mess off us,' a man's voice called weakly from below, and Kelly's heart seemed to almost stop. The voice was muffled but finally they could make out words. And the voice…the voice was surely Rafael's.

'Your Highness…' someone called.

'We're okay. Take your time. Get it right,' he called.

'Madame Henry?' The man beside Kelly—Heidi and Sophie's dad—could barely speak through tears as he called down to the schoolteacher they hoped was still safe.

'The children are all here.' The teacher must be elderly, Kelly thought. She sounded little and acerbic and frightened—and also just a wee bit bossy. 'Prince Rafael got down here just in time before the mess came down. When it started moving he blocked the door so it couldn't crash through but then the stuff moved again and he was caught...'

'Rafael was caught?' Kelly demanded, tugging loose debris free with her hands. They were so close...

'I'm fine,' Rafael called from through the rubble but she knew from his muffled voice that he wasn't.

'We have to get this free.'

'We take our time.' It was Sophie and Heidi's dad, pulling her back, putting both hands on her shoulders and setting her aside. 'We don't undo Prince Rafael's work—your work—by moving that slab until we're sure the land will hold.'

'Y-yes.'

'You've done enough,' he said gently and then looked at the seemingly impenetrable slab and sighed. 'And so have I. Everyone behind us is willing. We let those whose hearts aren't behind the slab make the decisions from now on.'

He was right. It nearly killed her but he was right. She was ushered out of the trench. Matty was waiting, staring at the entrance to the trench as if by will alone he could bring them out alive. She hugged him close. She was soaked to the skin, coated in thick, oozing mud. Women came forward carrying blankets. They would have ushered her away but she'd have none of it.

Rafael…Rafael…

But finally her prayers were answered. Finally the slab was moved. They inched it from its resting place with almost ludicrous caution, moving with so much care that it took them three long hours—hours when Matty and Kelly seemed to turn to stone.

But finally it was done. There was a growl of satisfaction as the trench stayed intact, that the shoring timbers held. And then the first child— a tiny girl, coated with thick, oozing clay, was handed up through the gap. She was grabbed by willing hands. A faint scream sounded behind them as the child was handed back, hand over hand, until she reached the end of the trench.

The last hands to reach her were her parents.

'Evaline,' a woman's voice said brokenly, and there was the sound of a man's hoarse sobs.

But those in the trench weren't hearing. Already more children were being handed out. Speed was of the essence here. This mass of mud and debris was unstable to say the least. It only needed one more earth tremor…

They had a chain operating. The children were being lifted out. There was no talking—just solid effort.

They seemed okay, Kelly thought, dazed. She'd left Matty with the women again and was at the neck of the trench where it narrowed down into the cavity under the slab. But she wasn't strong enough to be part of the chain handing back the children, so she slipped back to lean against the shoring timber and simply watched. Every face appearing at the hole under the slab she watched with terror. She'd forgotten to breathe. She'd forgotten to do anything.

So few injuries… There were cuts and bruises, but most of the children could put their arms up to be lifted. Most could cling to their rescuers. Most could reach out to their parents and sob and hold and sink into their parents' embrace as if they'd never let go.

One or two were hurt. There was one small boy with what looked like a broken arm. He whimpered as he was pulled out, but he still managed a smile when his mother whispered his name. There was an older boy with a nasty laceration to his cheek. 'I had to help Prince Rafael move the door,' he said with weak bravado, and it looked doubtful that he'd let such a wound be stitched. His parents were clasping him with pride and there was a shining pride in his own eyes. This was clearly a hero's wound. He'd helped his prince save the children.

Rafael…

Her heart was whispering the word, over and over. She glanced back along the line and saw Matty. His face was as white as hers. He was seeing all these happy endings but, like Kelly, he wanted his own.

She should ask. She should say to the boy with the cut face, What of Rafael?

She couldn't.

'That's twenty,' someone said in a gruff voice that wasn't quite concealing tears. 'Just the schoolteacher and the Prince to go.'

'You,' said a fierce woman's voice from under the slab, and the weary voice came in reply.

'When you're all out I'll be out but not before. Stop wasting time.'

'You're hurt.'

'Go!'

He was hurt. She'd known it. Dear God…

Hands were reaching up, small woman's hands. The schoolteacher was grasped and tugged free and hugged fiercely by the man who'd pulled her up.

'Romain, I have my dignity,' the little lady managed in between hugs and the men laughed and ignored her dignity and handed her back along the line as if she was also a child. As if she were made of the most precious porcelain…

And then… And then…

One hand came through the gap under the slab. A man's hand with a signet ring she recognized.

'Both hands,' the man at the front said, in a voice that was none too steady. 'We need a grip.'

'One hand.' Rafael's voice was muffled and pain-filled.

'You want us to come under and help?'

'No one comes under this slab. Get me out of here.'

'Rafael,' Kelly cried before she could help herself.

'Kelly,' Rafael muttered. 'What the hell are you doing here?'

'Come out and find out,' she whispered.

'Will we hurt you pulling you out?' someone asked him.

'A lot less than if this whole thing collapses.' His one hand was the only thing in sight and he pushed it higher. 'Pull.'

Each of the children and the schoolteacher too, had been lifted. But there was no one to lift Rafael. They were tugging him up by his one arm, holding his entire weight as they pulled.

He was hurt—badly hurt, Kelly thought, listening to his voice. But unless he'd let someone in to him...And he wouldn't. Their torches showed little—his mud-slicked face and blackness.

'Pull,' he ordered again and there was nothing to do but obey. And he came. He emerged into daylight with a savage groan, sliding out on to the floor of the trench and lying there, gasping for breath.

Kelly was in there, scrambling through the mud, on her knees, touching his face, scarcely able to breathe.

'Rafael.'

'Kell...' he gasped as she wiped mud from his eyes with her shirt, as she wept. 'Our magnificent

Princess Kellyn. Of course. A mine manager. I knew you'd make a magnificent princess.'

And then he passed out.

CHAPTER TEN

RAFAEL'S shoulder was dislocated. His leg was badly gashed. He'd be okay.

Officialdom took over. The little village had a very competent doctor and two efficient nurses. They carried him into the nearest intact house, put his shoulder back into place, stitched his leg, cleaned him up as much as they could and then ordered bedrest.

'When I'm back at the castle,' Rafael growled.

Kelly and Matty had been relegated to the background. They'd sat at the kitchen table while the women of the house plied them with soup and towels and as much comfort as they could. But Kelly's hands didn't stop shaking. She was holding Matty and she was aware that he was trembling as well.

He needed his nursery, she thought. He needed Marguerite and Ellen and Laura. He was clinging to her; she was his mama, but he needed the familiarity of home to ground him.

Home. The castle. The royal palace of Alp de Ciel.

They couldn't get a car there. 'But I'm thinking a horse and cart,' the doctor said.

'I'll ride,' Rafael countered, but the doctor looked at him as if he were crazy.

'A horse and cart it is,' Kelly said, and thus half an hour later the royal family made its way in somewhat less than royal state—a sturdy carthorse leading the way, tugging a small haycart. The haycart was filled with mattresses and pillows. Rafael complained every inch of the way but he had a nurse who looked like Brunhilda the Great by his side, there were two burly farmers leading the horse and clearing rocks from their path as they went, and he had no choice but to submit.

Kelly brought up the rear, riding her lovely mare. Matty, whose bravado had disappeared about the time Rafael had been declared safe, had crumpled into a little boy again. He was cradled before her, almost a part of her, clinging as close as he could get. His own horse and Rafael's stallion were being led behind.

It was like a scene from hundreds of years ago,

Kelly thought, dazed. A wounded prince returning from battle, his lady following behind.

Rafael's lady…

For that was what she was, she thought wearily as she followed the steady hoof-beats before her. Rafael's lady. Some time in the last few dreadful hours that was what she'd become.

Princess to Rafael's Prince.

Princess to this country.

'I thought you couldn't ride,' Matty whispered. Some time this dreadful day his allegiance had shifted as well. She was suddenly his mother. Yes, she'd always been that, but in his eyes she'd also been one of many people who'd flitted through his five years. Laura and Crater had been caught up at the hospital. Without his aunt, he'd needed someone to hold him, and that someone was his mother.

'I can ride,' she whispered into his hair. 'I chose not to because I was fearful of taking risks. But today…I think risks are something to be faced with courage. Not stupid risks, but those risks that need to be faced. Like being a part of this royal family.'

'You want to be royal?' He twisted a little, trying to see her face. 'But you can't be royal if you live in an attic.'

'Maybe it's time I came out of my attic,' she whispered. 'Maybe it's time I started to live. Maybe…maybe I need to think about putting on that dress.'

The nurse and the housekeeper whisked Rafael away as soon as they arrived at the castle. Ellen and Marguerite clucked over Kelly and Matty in concern. They were washed. Their bruises and scratches were anointed with care. Kelly tucked a cleaned and fed Matty into bed and watched him close his eyes before he even reached the pillows.

She was exhausted but there was no way she was heading for her bed. She made her way though the vast passages to the north tower—the tower where the ruling prince had his suite of private apartments.

When Rafael had arrived here after Kass's death he'd been horrified to find he was expected to use them. Crater had told her that, but he'd also told her, 'Prince Rafael has accepted he'll do what needs to be done. He can't be a part-time prince.'

So he was ensconced in state. She, however, was dressed in her jeans again, clean but faded. She needed to do something about her clothes, she thought.

Tomorrow. It was hardly the time for royal gowns tonight.

But for now…

Rafael.

She stood at the vast oak doors leading into his suite and felt almost shy. She'd never been in these rooms. By the time Kass had brought her to the castle he'd long since stopped wanting her.

Such memories… They were of a different person, she thought. A child bride. A girl who'd fallen in love with royalty before she knew what it was.

She knew what it was now. She also knew that as soon as she opened this door there'd be no going back.

She'd turned her back on royalty once before. Yes, it had been Kass who'd shunned her, but if there'd been a choice… Yes, she would have fled. She would have taken her small son with her but still she would have fled.

Rafael was right through this door. Rafael, who had almost as much call as she to hate royalty but who'd accepted his responsibilities; his duty.

Anna would go on with the merchandising of

his toys, Kelly thought. Rafael would still be able to develop them, but his life had changed. The wealthy Manhattan bachelor had accepted his heritage.

This wasn't her heritage, but she loved Matty and because she loved Matty she'd come back to the castle.

And because she loved Rafael, she'd stay.

All she had to do was tell him.

Such a little thing.

It was so hard to open the door.

'Open the door or go back to your attics,' she told herself sternly. 'Go on, Kelly. You can do it.'

'Princess Kelly,' she whispered back to herself. 'Princess Kellyn Marie de Boutaine. Open the door, stupid.'

His bed was enormous—the size of a small room! The four-poster bed was hung with acres of rich velvet curtains tied back with vast gold ropes and tassels. The eiderdowns were in matching crimson and purple and gold, as were the mountains of pillows at the end of the bed.

For a moment she couldn't see that anyone was in the bed.

'Kelly?' a loved voice said and she stilled.

'H-Hi. If you want to sleep I can come back later.'

'You're here,' he said in sleepy satisfaction. 'They've given me painkillers. They're making me woozy. Tell me I'm not dreaming. Tell me we got all those kids out and you're here.'

She crossed to the bed in a little run, and then stopped short—absurdly self-conscious.

'We got every single kid out,' she said unsteadily. 'And the schoolteacher. And you. Rafael, you might have been killed.'

'We got 'em out,' he said in sleepy satisfaction and his hand came out and caught her wrist and held. Hard. 'What's the final toll?'

'Six,' she whispered. 'All elderly people who couldn't get out of the way fast enough—the slip made a huge noise on the way down and most people were outside anyway.'

'Injuries?'

'None life-threatening. We've been lucky.'

'And elsewhere?' His voice was hoarse with worry. Kelly sank into the chair beside the bed, put her hand up to his face and traced his cheekbone with her finger.

'It was a minor earth tremor,' she whispered. 'There's little damage apart from in the village.

There's been some road damage near the border but nothing major. It was only the recent deforestation of the hillside that caused the slip.'

'Kass should never have allowed…'

'You will never allow,' she said strongly. 'It's your call now, Rafael.'

'We will never allow,' he said, his voice strengthening.

'You'll turn the country into a democracy?' she asked, wondering. It was what the other three Alp countries had done—altered the constitution so the monarchy was a titular head only.

'Of course, but that's not what I meant when I said *we*,' he said, and his hold on her wrist tightened.

Her heart stilled.

'Rafael…'

'Kelly,' he said and he smiled.

She gazed down at him. Her battered hero. His face was a mass of scratches and bruises. A long, thin scratch ran from ear to chin. The doctor had put a couple of stitches in the lower reaches. They'd cleaned him as much as they could but he wasn't fit yet for a full shower so his hair was still spiked with mud.

She loved him with all her heart.

'I love you,' he said and her heart restarted. If it was possible for a heart to sing, it sang now. She could hear it. A heart full of nightingales.

'I guess I love you too,' she said unsteadily. 'All the time you were under that slab…'

'You love me?'

'Maybe it's fear. Maybe.'

'Maybe nothing,' he growled. 'The guys tell me it was your skill that had them tunnelling in so professionally. We were lucky the whole thing didn't come down on us.'

It had. She didn't tell him that but he'd learn it anyway. Just after they'd pulled Rafael out, a final tremor had come through. The mass of mud had settled again, and their basement refuge had turned into what would have been a mass grave.

She shivered.

'Damn,' he said and struggled to sit up.

'Rafael, no.'

'Then lie down beside me,' he said, his voice gaining strength. 'A man's got to say what a man's got to say. Dammit, I should go down on bended knee.'

On bended knee…

'I don't think any of us are capable of bending for quite a while,' she whispered, and amazingly she heard herself chuckle. His tug was insistent. Well, what the heck. She hauled back the covers, wiggled in and lay down beside him.

He pulled her as close as he could, he turned his face to hers and he kissed her.

Fourth kiss? It was the best, she decided. It was the best by a country mile. It was a kiss of release of terror. It was a kiss of love. It was a kiss of promise.

'You know we can't go further,' he said, his voice laced with passion as finally he let her go. Only an inch, mind, but release her he did. 'I'm so full of drugs…'

'And you need to sleep.'

'Sleep be damned,' he said. 'Kelly, will you marry me?'

'Yes.'

'Just like that?'

'Just like that.'

'It's putting you in the royal goldfish bowl again,' he said, holding her close.

'But I'll be in it with you,' she whispered. 'And with Matty. If it's a goldfish bowl with you guys or a big wide world without, it's a no-brainer.'

'I'm your second prince.'

'Kass was no prince,' she said scornfully. 'He

might have been born royal but he never earned the title. You, however… You're prince through and through.'

'I'm a toy-maker.'

'And an equestrian,' she said, snuggling against him. He was wearing pyjamas. Self striped, flannel pyjamas. They'd have to go, she thought. Maybe not right now, though. A girl should show some restraint in the face of an injured hero.

He'd asked her to marry him!

'I guess riding again wasn't so bad,' he admitted.

'Your father loved it.'

'My father would have loved you.'

'My son loves you already.'

'Kelly,' he murmured and the strength had left his voice again. He had been heavily sedated to put his shoulder back in, she knew. He should be asleep.

'Yes, my love?'

'We can be a family?'

'Yes.'

'A royal family?'

'I'll even wear a tiara,' she teased and the hand around her waist tightened.

'Kelly?'

'Mmm.'

'I'm probably not capable of anything at all…'

'No, but…'

'No, but I can try,' he said. 'You know I asked you to marry me?'

'Yes.'

'And if a thing's promised then it's as good as done—right?'

'I guess,' she said dubiously, not sure where this was going.

'Then I have a wife,' he said in sleepy satisfaction. 'I have a princess. And, as a princess, as a wife, there are certain duties you'll be expected to face.'

'I…I guess.'

'Then we might as well start now,' he said, resigned.

'Um…right.' She thought about it. She twisted and pushed herself up so she was looking down into his beloved face. He was smiling. He was even laughing! And the look in his eyes…

It was a very royal look. It was a look of complete seduction.

'I only have one good arm,' he whispered as he tugged her down to him. 'Kelly, my love, my princess, my wife, I need help right now.'

'To do…to do what?'

'To take off these pyjamas!'

* * *

As coronations went it was magnificent.

Crater, as Secretary of State of Alp de Ciel, had been to the coronations in each of the Alp countries. He'd watched with wonder and with outright envy as the new generation of royals had taken their places as leaders in their countries, leading the way to prosperity for all.

They were here now. Prince Raoul of Alp d'Azuri was here, with the Princess Jessica, with their little son Edouard and with their twin daughters, Nicky and Lisle. Prince Maxsim of Alp d'Estella was in the next pew, with his Pippa and Marc and Sophie and Claire and bump. Prince Nikolai of Alp de Montez, with his beloved Princess Rose, with no bump as yet, were free to be best man and matron of honour. There might be no bump, but by the way they were looking at each other Crater knew the succession of Alp d'Estella was assured.

As it was assured here in Alp de Ciel. For this coronation was also a wedding.

'I'm damned if we're dragging all these dignitaries here twice,' Rafael had decreed. 'You say the coronation has to take place almost immediately. That's how Kelly and I feel about our wedding. Besides, Anna will kill me if I drag her away from New York twice in a month, and I'm tired of her yelling at us. So we combine.'

So combine they did. The vast and ancient cathedral in Alp de Ciel's capital was full to bursting. Every dignitary worthy of the name was crammed in, plus representatives of all walks of life in Alp de Ciel. The staff from the diggings in Australia sent representatives, beaming with approval at this happy ending for a loved staff member. Pete, as senior representative, was giving the bride away. Even Rafael's work team from Manhattan was here—his disabled staff—as many as could fly over. Rafael was planning a local workforce with the same background. It was an outward sign of the changes that were already sweeping the country.

'For this government is *of the people, for the people, by the people,* starting now,' Rafael and Kelly had decreed, and Crater agreed entirely. Their attitude meant a motley guest list, but so what? Royalty was changing for the better, in ways Crater could only wonder at.

Everywhere Crater looked there was approval— and no more so than at the end of the aisle where one small page-boy was holding a ring, waiting impatiently for Kelly and Rafael to need it.

Matty had reacted with joy to the news of Rafael and Kelly's engagement, whooping and bouncing with an excitement that made him seem less of a Crown Prince and more of a little boy with the world at his feet. From the time of the landslip the castle seemed to be tumbling with new life and new puppies and a kid who'd been released from his royal imperatives.

His lessons from Crater had been quartered. 'For there's all the time in the world for Matty to learn his royal obligations,' Kelly had decreed. 'For the next twenty years, those obligations are the responsibility of his parents.'

His parents…

For Matty had parents now and he approved entirely. Rafael would be his father as well as Prince Regent. Matty thought that was the neatest thing in the whole world. In the mornings he bounced into bed with Kelly, hugging her tight, claiming to the world that he had a mother he loved.

His Aunt Laura was in the front pew, weeping into a still inevitably paint-spattered handkerchief. Matty couldn't figure that one out. Why was she crying? He was watching this wedding with joy and love and anticipation of a very good party.

If they'd just get on with it.

And so they did.

'With this ring I thee wed…'

Rafael took the ring from Matty and he placed it on his bride's finger. His bride…Kelly, who'd embraced the royal wedding with enthusiasm and love. Her dress was truly wondrous. She looked like an Elizabethan bride, a true royal princess. Her dragon train swept out behind her, the golden embroidery shimmering in the sunlight streaming through the ancient stained glass windows. She looked truly regal.

But she also looked like a woman in love. She smiled mistily up at her bridegroom and the whole cathedral seemed to dissolve.

There wasn't a dry eye in the house, Crater thought, wiping away a surreptitious tear himself. And then, as he thought of what approached—the formal joining of these four nations to become one mighty Federation, he abandoned trying and let his tears flow freely.

These four Princes with their brides…Who said love couldn't conquer all? he thought. Love was making a damned fine fist of conquering all, right here, right now.

And the next morning—the first morning of their married life—they started as they meant to go on. Prince Rafael and Princess Kellyn rode together at dawn.

For their wedding gifts to each other were horses. Blaze would be ridden and loved and cared for, as would the other horses in the stables, but Blaze had been a part of Kass's life. He belonged to Matty now.

Kelly and Rafael needed to find their own future.

So they'd stolen two days from the mad preparation for the wedding and they'd spent those days looking at horses. They'd found Kelly's mare first. She was a silky-coated two-year-old, a soft grey with white markings, fearless and gentle in equal measure. She'd been bred for sale, but the farmer who'd bred her couldn't bear to part with her. Until now.

When the word had gone out that the Princess Kellyn needed a horse, she'd been quietly proffered. Her name was Cher, meaning beloved, and she already was.

And for Rafael...Nero had taken longer to

'What about a gold-mine or two to dig?'

'Maybe that too,' she said serenely. 'And a library to catalogue.'

'Just as well we have a lifetime,' Rafael said with satisfaction and kissed her again, so deeply she felt herself melt in a pool of white-hot desire. 'So much to do, my love, and so much loving to fit in along the way.' He released her again with reluctance, and twisted on Nero to tug blankets free from his saddle-bags. He smiled across at her as he tossed them down on the lush pasture, his smile wicked and wanton and filled with pure, unadulterated lust.

'Maybe we should start now,' he said softly. 'For I doubt if a lifetime is long enough.'

MILLS & BOON PUBLISH EIGHT LARGE PRINT TITLES A MONTH. THESE ARE THE EIGHT TITLES FOR DECEMBER 2008.

———————— ✄ ————————

HIRED: THE SHEIKH'S SECRETARY MISTRESS
Lucy Monroe

THE BILLIONAIRE'S BLACKMAILED BRIDE
Jacqueline Baird

THE SICILIAN'S INNOCENT MISTRESS
Carole Mortimer

THE SHEIKH'S DEFIANT BRIDE
Sandra Marton

WANTED: ROYAL WIFE AND MOTHER
Marion Lennox

THE BOSS'S UNCONVENTIONAL ASSISTANT
Jennie Adams

INHERITED: INSTANT FAMILY
Judy Christenberry

THE PRINCE'S SECRET BRIDE
Raye Morgan

™MILLS & BOON®
Pure reading pleasure™

1108 Rom LP